Short Stories

TALES OF REALITY AND IMAGINATION

Rachel Costantino

CLAIREMONT BOOKWORKS

San Diego, California

CLAIREMONT BOOKWORKS
P.O. Box 179191
San Diego, CA 92177
www.clairemontbookworks.com

Publisher's Note: This is a work of fiction. Names, characters, places, and incidents are a product of the author's imagination. Locales and public names are sometimes used for atmospheric purposes. Any resemblance to actual people, living or dead, or to businesses, companies, events, institutions, or locales is completely coincidental.

Book Layout ©2013 BookDesignTemplates.com

Ordering Information:
Quantity sales. Special discounts are available on quantity purchases by corporations, associations, and others. For details, contact the "Special Sales Department" at the address above.

Short Stories / Rachel Costantino — 1st Edition
Printed in the United States of America

20 19 18 17 16 15 14   1 2 3 4 5 6

ISBN 978-0-9912265-0-4

This book is dedicated to my husband Ralph because he actually liked the stories, to our daughter Kathy, two sons David and Damon, and to our granddaughters Dana, Chelsea, Desiree, Delia, Rachel and Deidre who opened up a world of magic love for me.

Can't

Can't say goodbye, just can't
I was there when you came into the world
I watched you grow
I laughed as you learned to walk and talk
I watched you grow
I saw the miracle of you
I watched you grow
You're in my heart, in my soul
Can't say goodbye, just can't.

—RACHEL COSTANTINO

Table of Contents

Acknowledgments

To Ralph, my life partner on earth and beyond, I owe a special acknowledgment for his encouragement and belief in me. As my cheerleader and initial copy editor, he drove me to a higher quality. To my son David, who worked diligently for many months to improve upon my original vision, I owe many thanks for giving his time as a developmental editor and publisher, and for never giving in when he knew he could clarify my thinking and structure. Next, I would like to express my gratitude to Deb Eaton for her help with the design and layout of the book cover. It is magnificent. Finally, to my line editing superstar, Carissa Joy Johnson, I give my heartfelt thanks. She meticulously addressed spelling, punctuation and grammar, in addition to shortening and rearranging my sentences, all for the better. She made suggestions to help bring my characters alive. Not only did Carissa gently improve my punctuation, but she also let me know when she liked or was moved by a particular story, which encouraged me tremendously. Carissa Joy was indeed a joy throughout the entire process.

Introduction

You are about to embark upon a journey of reality and imagination. All of the characters depicted herein, have their basis in reality. However, as to their thoughts and emotions, well, that's where the imagination comes in. From animals in *Ceramics?*, to gnomes in *Mr. McElhaney*, and trolls in *The Scent of Lilacs*, you will briefly suspend reality and embrace a magical and enchanting world of imagination.

In *Christmas Stocking Hooks*, you will meet six little girls as they experience the joy of Christmas. In *A Teeny Tiny Story*, you meet a "valley girl" dog named Ella. In *The Beginning, Cheerio Tears, Unfinished*, and *Earp*, you will experience the joys and sorrows of life. The adventures of many animals, domestic and wild, occur in the following stories: *Sally and Harry, We Said—She Said, The Liberated Feline* and *Granny, Maggie Mae and Shadrach*.

In *Two Weeks Out of Time*, you will glimpse inside the hallucinations, confusion and pain experienced by a cyclist, as he awakens from a long coma after a horrific motorcycle accident. *Norman and Mikie* takes you along on a real-life escapade, where a cat named Norman Bates escapes from captivity only to find himself living a harsh life on the outside. His return from the wearisome life of a wanderer takes him right back to the people and place he abandoned two weeks earlier.

Finally, in *I Remember*, you'll encounter a true love story. Follow along on a woman's lifelong fascination with a young seventeen year old boy, who then becomes a man, and learn of the joy they share together, the pride, the love, and even their parting grief.

These are merely a few of the delightful people and creatures you will encounter while reading this inspiring volume. Now, let's get started with *The Beginning*.

THE BEGINNING

Biology is the least of what makes someone a mother.

—OPRAH WINFREY

Then There Were Three

They were young. He was so handsome he was almost pretty; she carried the bloom of youth like all young girls. Anxiety showed on their faces, their hands clutched tightly together as if to buffet a strong wind. They faced a drab, undecorated building fronting onto a busy, noisy street. The couple loitered momentarily outside the wide door. She timidly looked up and questioned him with her eyes. "Yes," he said, "we're going to do it, we have to. We can't stop now; we've gone too far already to worry about consequences." Anguished, she softly replied, "But what about the mother?" He pulled her into his arms harshly and told her, "You're the mother now, only you." He opened the door and nudged her into the building.

They walked warily down the empty, quiet hall. Stopped once on their stealthy journey by a curious woman in white, they were allowed to continue. Halting in front of an open doorway, he looked around carefully before leading her into the barren, almost empty room where a tiny baby lay in a small bed wrapped in a soft blue blanket.

She quickly looked around the room as though frightened that someone would stop her before she bent to the baby. She turned to the thin young man and he smiled at her in encouragement. "Go ahead and pick him up." She replied, "But what if he cries?" "He won't—he already loves you—look at him." With tears in her eyes, she took the tiny baby in her arms.

"Can we really do this? Just walk out with him? He belongs to someone else." "No," said the young man, "he's yours. I promised you a baby and this one is yours." As she watched the baby hungrily, his small hand reached out to touch her face and she tightened her hold. "Right now, let's go. I'm ready," she told him fiercely.

As they walked down the long hallway, this time with a life in their arms, they walked quickly. It was too easy; surely someone would stop them. The walk seemed to take much longer than when they entered. Still, there was no one to stop them as they reached the outer door.

The young couple walked out into the sunlight with the small bundle held firmly. And still, there was no one to stop them. The girl whispered softly as she held him tightly in her arms, "You belong to me now and I'll never give you up, never." It really was true.

A sensation of wild elation spread through both of them. They had done it!

Suddenly feeling as though he carried the weight of the world on his shoulders, the young man stopped briefly before journeying into the sunlight with his wife. He turned to gaze at the woman in white. Nodding encouragement as she stood in the doorway of the drab building, she smiled and closed the door. His eyes flickered upward toward the sign above, SAN DIEGO COUNTY ADOPTION, and then he turned and followed his family into the rest of their lives. For now they were a family.

CERAMICS?

The world of reality has its limits; the world of imagination is boundless.

—JEAN-JACQUES ROUSSEAU

Prologue

Have you ever looked at ceramic animals and wondered about their world? Can they see and hear? Do they think? Do they even have a world? Are they aware? My ceramic animals are very much aware; they see, they hear, they think; and within their world, they lead a very lively existence. Of course, they must imagine their activities, because they are, after all, ceramic. And their conversations are, by necessity, imaginary and unheard by any but themselves, but when active with one another, their minds blend in a most remarkable way.

Chapter One

Cat was a ceramic "piggy" bank. Most of her time was spent alone, sitting near a huge window in a large bedroom. She spent her day imagining the cleaning and grooming of her beautiful little body. Cat wasn't distressed that she had to imagine her movements because it was all she had ever known. Cat thought all important people lived her way.

Cat started her cleaning and grooming at the top of her head. She imagined a lick to her right paw and a swipe of that paw over the top of her head; then a lick to the left paw and a swipe with it over the top of her head. Next the ears would be scratched and cleaned, the right one first (because Cat was, of course, right-handed), then a vigorous licking of the chest starting from the right and swiping all the way around to the left, which resulted in a very good exercise in cleaning. All this imagined exercising left her just a bit tired, so a short cat nap would follow, especially if the sun's rays had started to beam into the window. Cat didn't know that she couldn't curl up, so she just enjoyed the sun as it poured over her little hard ceramic body.

After her cat nap, Cat's clever mind would start again on the cleaning and grooming—only this time she started with the hind legs. First the right leg would go straight out and she licked all of the way from the foot up to the body. This took some time because she always did a good job and she was very careful to clean the little tufts of hair that grew between her toes. Then the left leg shot straight out and the process would be repeated. Sometimes she cleaned her tummy area next and sometimes her sides came next. This way Cat never got bored with the grooming. It was, after all, her body and she took the task seriously.

Cleaning her tail was an absolute joy because Cat could imagine how it switched all around, and then she would lick it all over and up and down. Owning a tail was pure delight, and Cat knew she was the most beautiful creature that God had created. The hardest part of cleaning and grooming was Cat's back because she just couldn't imagine how it could be reached. She knew it was there and she knew it should be cleaned, but how to reach it was a puzzle.

By the way, Cat did know there were other creatures in the world because she didn't live alone; Woman and Man lived in her home from early evening until early morning. Cat was left to her own devices all through the day. This was good planning because Cat's private life was very important; Woman and Man would have been an intrusion to her daily routine. Cat's life was perfect.

Grooming was usually interrupted three to four times each day with cat naps so when Woman came home Cat was rested and eager for the conversations that took place. Sometimes Man came home early, but he didn't pay attention to Cat, so Cat liked it when Woman came home first. Some humans are sensitive to the real world of ceramic creatures and Woman was very sensitive to Cat. Woman belonged to Cat. Almost every evening when she came home she patted Cat's head and gently touched the freckle on Cat's nose. Woman always spoke her mind openly when she first arrived home and it was an enjoyable interlude to listen to all her chatter about her daily routine. Woman was with other humans throughout the day and she liked most of them, so the patter was gentle and informative. Humans were a curious species and personally, Cat was thankful that she was feline.

Chapter Two

Late one summer day, Man arrived home burdened and noisy. He carried a large box and he was excited about something. Man was always pleasant but not particularly mindful of Cat. On this day, he came in talking loudly to both Woman and Cat. He put down his box, tore open the lid and reached in, pulling out something wrapped in tissue paper. He uncovered a colorful creature the likes of which Cat had never seen; it wasn't human and it wasn't feline.

Man was talking excitedly and he called this creature a dog. Man had always wanted a Bassett Hound but, because they lived in a condominium, animals were forbidden. Woman was delighted and immediately, the thing was placed mere inches from Cat. If Cat could have openly hissed, she would have. As it was, she was having an enormous imaginary hissy fit. For a reason that even Cat couldn't have explained, the entry of this dog into her aura was not tolerable. Dog was as excited as Cat but for another reason. He was thrilled to see Cat because he had been very frightened. Man had taken Dog from his shelf-home in the gift shop and placed him in that box, and it had been scary in there.

Dog knew all about cats because he had lived in the gift shop on his shelf-home for some time. There were cats, dogs, birds and several other types of creatures living there with him. Dog hadn't actually talked with a cat because he had been too busy imagining himself chasing the birds, but he was aware of cats. Cat, however, was horrified by this bumptious thing being introduced into her quiet space. Even another cat would have been intolerable but this … this … DOG, was unspeakable.

Cat imagined herself hissing and spitting viciously; Dog immediately understood the problem. However, he knew he could win her over because you see, Dog was a gentleman. The only creatures that drove him over the brink were birds. He just couldn't be rational around birds. But this can be discussed later; right now he had a feline problem. By the way, Dog was not a "piggy bank," but he was ceramic.

Woman was delighted with Man's solution to a problem that had plagued them for some time. Man hadn't been able to relate to Cat, and this bothered Woman because she knew that everyone needed a way to unburden themselves; Woman cleared her thinking with Cat when she came home in the evening before Man came in. The one-sided conversations with Cat left Woman unclouded and eager for the evening ahead with Man. But Man didn't speak to Cat at all, and this had bothered Woman because she knew that he loved animals; he just didn't seem to love Cat. Of course, Cat wasn't bothered, because Cat knew she was beloved, mostly by herself.

Dog's first evening with Man was busy, loud and cheerful. Dog, too, was making loud barking noises and was panting and drooling. If Cat had been able to move she would have been shuddering at this loathsome horror. Woman couldn't hear Cat, but Cat heard Woman. And Cat heard Dog and that awful barking noise he made. And he smelled strange too. What on earth did he get fed to make that awful odor? Cat couldn't get over her horror.

Cat was very glad when Woman and Man started preparing for bed because she was exhausted, but to her disgust, Dog stayed by her side. It appeared she had another roommate.

Chapter Three

As Dog awoke early the next morning, he was immediately aware of his new surroundings. He was accustomed to being awakened by the birds in the gift shop where he lived, but this morning, all was peaceful. He sat quietly trying to adjust to the lack of bird song. He remembered the man who had picked him up placing him in the dark, scary box. But as he remembered the man and the woman who lifted him from the box, he also remembered his excitement at being placed near a beautiful ceramic cat. He eagerly turned his eyes to the cat sleeping peacefully. He knew she was sleeping because he could feel her quiet snoring. He looked around his new surroundings. It was still dark but he could make out the outlines of Woman and Man sleeping.

So this was a home. He had often wondered about a home when his gift shop friends left, one-by-one, for new homes. Now he had a home and he was eager for the first day of his new life to start. He was so excited that he started his imaginary whimpering and he thought he saw Cat's eyes snap open. Actually, they were open already, since Cat and Dog were ceramic, but Dog imagined that they snapped open. Cat's immediate, imaginary reaction was to hiss, then to growl while her hairs stood on end. But Cat quieted down. She just sat there and warily eyed Dog. Dog expected exactly this reaction. Remember, he had seen many animals come and go from his old home; he had lots of experience.

Dog sat quietly while Cat watched him. He knew what he was doing, but Cat was a novice at this friendship thing, so Dog waited for Cat to calm down.

They watched each other cautiously but peacefully for some time until Dog asked quietly what time the people usually woke up. Cat didn't answer for a while, but finally told him it would be just before sunup. So they sat watching each other some more. Finally, Woman and Man started stirring and Dog was eager to have them talk to him. Cat was simply bored with the whole thing and sat purring to herself. To show her contempt, she started cleaning her front paws and then her tail. Cat's tail always fascinated her so she quickly lost herself in the pleasure of imagined switching and cleaning.

Man, remembering his new pleasure, jumped out of bed, patting the top of Dog's head as he walked by. Dog was deliriously happy at this show of affection: so much that Cat contemptuously told him to control himself, please. Dog was delighted that Cat spoke to him, so he asked her the daily routine. Cat spicily told him her own beloved routine and told him that he could use some cleaning too because he didn't smell good. This was news to Dog because it was his opinion that his smell was interesting. But he decided to let Cat's comment pass.

To Dog's dismay, Woman and Man spent very little time at home in the morning and that time was used running back and forth dressing and straightening the room. Dog did get a few scratches and pats, but not nearly enough to set his mind at rest, so by the time the house quieted down he was whimpering again. Since Dog was a Bassett Hound, when he was sad, he bayed. In his imagination he was baying grandly. Cat was aghast at this deplorable sound and made up her mind that she would ignore it. But the baying went on and on and on. So she snapped at Dog to STOP IT! And, of course, he did. Dog was very agreeable; he simply needed company.

To keep the noise down, Cat asked Dog where he came from and who he lived with. This was flattering to Dog so he started from Day One and recounted all his experiences with all the animals in his old gift shop. After the third sentence, Cat was busy cleaning and grooming so she heard no more, but Dog didn't notice until Cat had finished grooming her tummy and went to sleep. This hurt Dog's feelings, so he started howling again. Cat leaped to her feet and hushed him again. It was becoming obvious that Dog was going to need much more attention than Cat was prepared to give.

So Cat told Dog that he too should clean and groom himself. Dog was always prepared to cooperate with anything reasonable, so he started licking his front paws. When he reached his hind paws (again, in his mind, of course), he found interesting debris between his toes: a small rock and a piece of gum. Dog wondered out loud where it could have come from. Cat was so exasperated that she bit her own tail and it hurt. This caused a rift in the new friendship because it was one-sided anyway. Cat turned away from Dog and went to sleep. Of course, you know what this caused: that's right, Dog started whimpering and then howling.

Cat awoke with a spit and a hiss. The friendship was off to a rocky start and Cat was becoming frustrated and tired too, because by this time of day she should have been half clean and she should have had three uninterrupted cat naps.

Dog watched all Cat's writhing and hissing with amusement because he knew exactly what he was doing. He knew that Cat would—out of necessity—break down and like him because she had no other choice. They were sitting inches apart and that was that! He would not be ignored.

Chapter Four

Cat tried to be aloof for several weeks, and then became so accustomed to Dog's sweet silliness that, in spite of herself, she started liking the messy creature called Dog. They settled into a routine that was to her liking, even though her cleaning and grooming was constantly broken up with Dog's neediness. He was a loveable thing, and harmless, so she tried her best to soothe him and keep him happy.

It seemed to Cat that Dog was most needy during the day, but this might have been because Cat was accustomed to being absorbed with herself throughout the day. Nights were not so hard on Cat because evenings were shared with Woman and Man.

Cat was relieved of her Dog duties in the evening when Man came home and entertained him. Cat thought their relationship was curious because it involved Man pretending to toss things in the air and Dog wildly leaping for it and dropping it at Man's feet. Cat's understanding of friendship was for Woman to talk to her, smooth her fur and touch her nose freckle gently; Cat just sat peacefully and let Woman love her. All the noisy, busy activity from Man was bewildering and somewhat upsetting to her. The rowdiness was distressing. To Cat, Man was a mystery and so was Dog. What a curious situation!

During the day, Dog easily became bored and morose. This consumed more time than Cat was willing to give. But she had no choice. In her head she heard that horrible barking-baying sound. And when Dog was barking and baying, he also drooled. Ugh! What sort of beast was this? But to Cat's total confusion, she began to have feelings of compassion for this drooling mess. He was actually loveable. It was a new emotion for Cat because all her life she had been absorbed with only her own lovely being. She was surprised to have this sense of caring for a thing in such disarray.

Dog had always dreamed that when he left his gift shop shelf-home, it would be so wonderful because he would become important to someone. His new life was exactly what he had always wanted. Of course, he was left behind when Man went to work in the morning, but he had Cat to keep him company all day long. Cat quickly learned that the best way to keep Dog from baying was to talk with him. This meant opening up her heart and pouring out all her imaginary feelings of love for herself. As Cat talked about herself, she found that Dog was sympathetic and understanding. His tender, warm, listening stance touched her heart and she began to wonder about Dog. He patiently listened for weeks, until finally she asked him about his life in the gift shop with all the cats, dogs, birds and other animals. Cat was fascinated with Dog's story because she had never cared about anyone but herself. Dog was opening up a whole new experience for her. The ceramic animals that Dog spoke of apparently cared about each other and were interested in each other. This was an education for Cat and all this time she had only been trying to pacify Dog to keep him from drooling, whimpering and baying. Cat was entranced and finally, a real bond developed between the two—a firm friendship was formed.

Dog told her about the day his imagination had allowed a bird to land on the top of his head. It drove him almost berserk and he became frenzied. But the bird simply sat there until Dog finally realized that all he had to do was think the bird back in its cage. It took a lot of energy to do this but from the experience, Dog learned how strong he could be.

Chapter Five

Cat and Dog kept up a lively imaginary life. Cat taught Dog to clean himself and to stop whimpering and baying. And when Cat mentioned her own back cleaning problem, Dog suggested that she should imagine him licking it clean. It took some time for Cat to realign her thinking about Dog's abilities, not to mention his slurping tongue, but after some deep thinking on her part, she decided, why not? So Dog became a subtle part of Cat's cleaning routine. And now Cat's back, too, was clean. It did smell just a little bit different, but no matter. During the day, each was totally absorbed with the other and their evenings were full with their humans—life was near perfect.

Chapter Six

However, life never goes on the same for long, and as pleasant and interesting as life was to the two of them, it didn't last.

One harrowing morning, Cat and Dog awoke to a loud and noisy clamor. Woman and Man were rushing around in a manner that was not normal at all. Woman was pulling things out of drawers and Man was thrusting them into a small travel bag. The situation was chaotic and when Dog started his imaginary whimpering and then baying, Cat couldn't even try to stop him because she too was aghast: this had never happened before. Dog carried on in his desolate manner for what seemed to be hours and they were totally ignored by Woman and Man who soon left with the small bag; Cat was nearly cata-tonic. Finally, Cat became aware of Dog's condition and was horrified to see that Dog had been injured. In the dizzying fray something had landed on Dog's head and he had a chip in it; he looked dented.

Did I tell you that Dog was a Bassett Hound? He had beautiful, short brown hair with white spots around his body and a sort of long tail. His head had been all brown but now he had a large white spot chipped right into the top of his head. Cat, for the very first time in her life, wanted desperately to comfort someone other than her-self—she wanted to comfort Dog. Cat didn't know why there was so much confusion in their home on this day, but she did know that Dog needed her, so she started talking. She talked and talked and talked until finally Dog was able to listen to her. Cat told him of all her new feel-ings about his friends in the gift shop. Dog finally real-ized that Cat had been listening to him all this time. She had become entranced with his stories of his old life in the gift shop and all the other ceramic animals.

And on this long, long day, Cat told Dog about her own secret pain that didn't even exist until Dog came in-to her life, for she thought all ceramic animals were "pig-gy banks." Now she knew otherwise and she was mortified as she told him that people dropped money in-to the back of her head. She told Dog about quarters and nickels and dimes and pennies. And when she told him about silver dollars she started to giggle because silver dollars dropped right to the bottom of her body with a clunk and always gave her an imaginary burp! As she re-alized how absurd her own so-called pain was, she saw the silly looking white chip in the top of dog's head and started laughing. Dog started to laugh with her until both of them were shaking with giggles. They didn't stop until imaginary tears were pouring down their faces and only they could see each other's tears.

Chapter Seven

They were so engrossed in their stories to each other that the day passed quickly and late into the night Man finally came home alone and went straight to bed, without even noticing Dog's new head dent. Cat thought this distressing and really quite selfish of him. And where was Woman?

For two days this curious pattern was repeated and on the third day the door flew open and both Woman and Man were finally home together. Woman carried a small package and both Cat and Dog were alarmed, thinking it must be another ceramic animal. They were still getting to know each other, it was too soon for a new one, and anyway, their sun spot was only big enough for their two bodies.

Woman sat carefully on the bed holding the package while Man carried in one item after another. In the confusion no one paid any attention to Cat and Dog. They sat transfixed while Man put together a very small bed. Then Woman placed her package in the small bed and it moved! And it mewed! It was a cat! No, wait, Woman took it up again, unwrapped it, and it wasn't a cat; it was a tiny wiggling human. Dog was perplexed; he had seen all sorts of animals in his gift shop home, but never anything like this. Cat, however, saved the day because she had heard of this. She had never seen one but it did fit the description of a baby. She was able to ease Dog's mind and they both watched, fascinated, as Woman and Man consumed the afternoon with their attention totally on Baby.

It was late evening before Woman looked up and smiled at Cat and Dog, then leaped up in concern when she noticed the white dent in Dog's head, calling Man to come look. They anguished over how it must have happened on the day they were rushing to the hospital. Dog, by this time, had forgotten his dent and was delighted to have both of them petting him and rubbing his dent. He was just happy to have everyone back home again. And, too, it didn't hurt. Cat had helped him so much with all her caring for him that he was sort of happy to have something so unique as a dent in his head.

Chapter Eight

Of course, life was definitely not the same after Baby came into their lives. That's not to say it was unhappy; they were very happy, all five of them.

It was curious to Dog because in his mind he thought that Man's being occupied with someone other than Dog, should have meant loneliness, but it didn't work that way. Baby brought noise, clutter, confusion and happiness. Woman was still gentle with both Cat and Dog. Man still found time to pretend tossing things for Dog to imagine chasing. And now Baby was beginning to lie on the floor on a blanket watching Cat and Dog with large blue eyes that never seemed to blink. At first, Dog thought it might be ceramic because its eyes were so large and so still. But he finally agreed with Cat that it was, indeed, a human.

They all became so accustomed to the white dent in Dog's head that, after a while, it was simply another story in the pattern of their lives just as the old stories of Dog's gift shop friends, Cat's solitary lazy days of dream cleaning, Woman's days of working downtown in an office and Man's happy-go-lucky lounging all evening. Those days were long gone. Today was so busy there was just barely time for Cat, Dog and Woman to catch cat naps in their sun spots before Baby awoke and Man came home in the evening. But life was good.

Epilogue

Is there a moral to this story, you ask? Well, no. But Cat came to treasure Dog and his loving anecdotes about his friends from the gift shop. And Dog finally found a friend who was steadfast in her devotion to him. Cat finally found an imaginary "scrub brush" for her back.

Is this the end of the story, you ask? Well, of course not. Several years later, Baby Two came along and all through the growing years of the two children, Cat and Dog became more and more faded from the friendly sun that smiled through their window. Dog's chipped head was only the first of many chips on both their bodies. These signs of joyful, robust life didn't bother either of them because of the happy laughter that filled their home.

Dog was never lonely again, and Cat almost never got an uninterrupted cat nap—not for many, many years—but she didn't mind. They continued their lively imaginary conversations that could be heard only by each of them. No one else was aware of their secret lives, not even the children who had a magical life of their own, but as they say, "that's a whole 'nother story."

CHRISTMAS STOCKING HOOKS

Joy delights in joy.

—WILLIAM SHAKESPEARE

Making Memories

Once upon a time, in the year 1985, Grandpa Costantino sat pondering his fireplace; something was missing. The fireplace mantle shelf looked barren. Christmas was coming, and his large family would soon descend on his new home for a joyous celebration of The Christ Child's birth. True, the shelf could be covered in pine boughs and twinkling lights. But he wanted something meaningful. He looked, and he thought. He thought, and he looked. Tiny beads of perspiration popped from his brow.

Grandpa drifted off into a world of his own, thinking of all the granddaughters that would one day run through this house. Its size would accommodate many boisterous children. Already, there was Dana, who was always filled with high spirits. The thought of her sturdy little body and bright mind brought a smile to his face. What a busy little person. How many more granddaughters would bless his family?

His granddaughter Chelsea's worried little brow then came to mind. She always appeared to be so thoughtful, seeming to carry the world on her shoulders. She would be a thinker – and why not? Chelsea's mother had worried over things all her life. He smiled as he remembered

Chelsea's mother's potato bug "friends." She had been captivated by their roly-poly bodies as they rolled into balls. She named all her potato bugs Susie and her Susie bugs were worried over and attended to carefully for several months until she finally lost interest. He also remembered trying to talk Chelsea's mother out of running away from home when she was a little girl. Arguing made nary a dent in her determination, until Grandpa said the family dog couldn't go with her. When given that piece of information, she thoughtfully changed her mind, unpacked her bag and decided to stay home with the dog.

There was something about his youngest granddaughter Desiree that seemed to say, "I am me, and I am strong." Grandpa smiled to himself, thinking of her recent noisy and indignant howl of displeasure at being frustrated over some small thing. He clearly remembered Desiree's father's identical reaction to frustration when he was small. They were much alike and, small as she was, and though she had been in his life mere months, Grandpa knew Desiree was to be his brave heart. How many more granddaughters would bless his family?

He knew there would be more and that each of them would be different, one from the other. Maybe the next granddaughter would be a timid little soul with a soft heart. She might cry easily, allowing him to tease her while they watched sad movies. He had room for many more granddaughters in his heart, and so did his house.

He hoped that one of his granddaughters would be a rowdy hoyden who jumped and ran and yelled. The house was large enough; the extra wide hallway was just right for rambunctious children. He made a note to himself to make a deal with his son and daughter to let the little girls run and play at will, even a little wildly at times.

Finally, he needed a giggling little girl that would listen to his stories, someone who would sit on his lap and listen as long as he cared to talk. Grandpa got a little tear in his eye. "Whoa," he thought, "this has gone far enough! John Wayne wouldn't tear up thinking of granddaughters—enough of this!"

His mind continued to drift, and he smiled to himself realizing he thought only of granddaughters; granddaughters now and granddaughters to come. "Why not grandsons?" he wondered in puzzlement.

All of a sudden, his face lit up with a huge smile. He jumped up. "I've got it. I know what to do and Grandma will love it."

And, so, once (again) upon a time, in the year 1985, Grandpa set about gathering his materials. There were to be six little brass hooks. Each little hook would be secured to the bottom of the fireplace shelf. As the group of little brass hooks grew in number, they became more and more excited. They had been gathering, one by one, for several days. None of the little hooks knew that their only purpose would be to hold Christmas Stockings through the Christmas Season.

When they were completely assembled, the group of six little brass hooks knew something would happen soon. During the assembly process, Grandpa dropped each new hook into the group. The oldest in the group was Hook One; then Hook Two, Hook Three, Hook Four, Hook Five, and finally, Hook Six.

Hook One was just a teeny bit self-important because she was the oldest—ten whole days older, you see. She chattered continuously to each newcomer as they were dropped, one-by-one, into a small pile on the fireplace shelf in the huge living room. As the pile grew, Hook One became more and more protective of her little companions, one might even say, sort of "motherly."

The shelf was rather high above the floor, and Hook Two got dizzy each time she thought of falling off. She worried so about her dizziness that she stopped looking over the edge.

Hook Three, however, was very brave. She offered to drop herself from the shelf, just to show Hook Two that she shouldn't worry so. Hook Three was convinced that she would bounce right back up to the shelf. The mere idea that someone would drop from such a height, so unnerved Hook Four, that the offer was withdrawn. Hook Five roared to life with a burst of energy yelling over her shoulder at the others. "Come on, let's explore this place!"

Hook Six giggled herself into the hearts of her five companions. She had absolutely no fears, knowing very well that all the older hooks would take good care of her. So Hook Five and Hook Six ran up and down the shelf with great abandon, and with an abundance of loud fun.

The subject of the hooks' most energetic conversation was what was to be their purpose in life? Hook One felt they must be meant for something very important. Naturally, because she was the oldest, she would be the most important hook for whatever their task was to be. Hook Two was certain that she would be called upon to sit on the edge of the shelf holding up the others so they could dangle dangerously as they gripped their burdens. This, considering her difficulty with dizziness, gave her much to worry about. Hook Three bravely assured her fretting companion, Hook Two, "Not to worry, I'll be there to help." Hook Four, nervous nelly that she was, couldn't handle the conversations. She buried herself under the others when the subject of their purpose was discussed. Hook Five and Hook Six joyously careened around the shelf, taking no part in the serious conversations.

When Grandpa's gentle hands carefully gathered the six little hooks together, the pride, wooziness, bravado, nervousness and sheer merriment of all six was stilled. They were on their way, at last.

To the agitation of the others, Hook One was briefly separated from the group. The five little hooks watched with cautious fascination as their friend was gently picked up by her top, lowered to the bottom of the shelf, and, curiously, twisted around and around for a time. For the first time in her short life, Hook One was speechless. Hook Two was picked up and treated identically to her older friend, as were Hook Three, Hook Four, Hook Five and Hook Six, until all were twisted in a line into the lower edge of the fireplace shelf.

Hook One, being twisted into place first, felt quite important in her spot furthest on the left. Hook Two was so dizzy after all the twisting that she had almost no feeling left. Hook Three's bravery was severely tested, practically to her limit. Hook Four, placed a couple of feet away from the other three, was almost in tears by the time her twisting was completed. She was quickly comforted though, when Hook Five and Hook Six were placed nearby, yelping cheerfully through the whole experience. Their delight was so contagious that by the time all six were secure beneath the shelf, their conversation was nonstop.

Grandma Costantino walked into the room just as Grandpa twisted the last hook into place. She whooped in surprise and burst out, "Oh, what a wonderful idea. Won't everyone be surprised? Why so many? We only have three grandchildren. You did make them for hanging grandchildren's Christmas Stockings, didn't you?" Grandpa's response was naturally very reasonable because Grandpa was always very reasonable. "Yes, they're for grandchildren's Christmas Stockings, and yes, we only have three now, but there will be more over the years. We have to be prepared; after all, we expect to be here a long, long time."

And so, on that first Christmas in their new home, three brightly colored Christmas Stockings were hung with great care on Hook One, Hook Two and Hook Three. Grandpa was especially proud, because he had created a gift for his granddaughters, and that gift would be passed on to all future owners of his and Grandma's home. As long as the house was standing, these little brass Christmas Stocking Hooks would be treasured and passed on to each new owner over the years. But for now, Grandpa knew these little hooks would help build memories that would last lifetimes for his own granddaughters. And after all, building memories were what grandparents were for.

All the little hooks listened to Grandma and Grandpa with great excitement. Hook One would hold Dana's Christmas Stocking. The load might be heavy, because the stocking would be filled with Christmas delights. Hook Two was especially pleased that she would hold Chelsea's Christmas Stocking, for she liked the idea of bringing a smile to that worried little face. She vowed to herself that she would not look down; she would not allow herself to get dizzy holding Chelsea's Christmas Stocking. Hook Three bravely told herself that she could, she could, she could hold Desiree's Christmas Stocking, even though it might be heavy.

In the years that followed, on the day after Thanksgiving, all six little hooks were removed from their storage box and twisted into place under the fireplace shelf. Just as Grandpa predicted, their family was blessed with three more beautiful granddaughters, for a total of six. Once or twice, Grandpa thought it was curious that he had never imagined a grandson. Oh well, not to worry; granddaughters filled his life wonderfully.

Through the years, Hook One gave Dana much joy by holding up her Christmas burden. Hook Two never once got dizzy holding up her burden, and it became a Christmas favorite for Chelsea, whose little brow almost never furrowed on those wonderful Christmas holidays. Hook Three's stocking was plundered immediately on Desiree's arrival to visit Grandpa and Grandma on Christmas Eve. Hook Four was delighted with Delia's gentle probing for all the secrets held in her stocking each Christmas. Hook Five and Hook Six waited anxiously for several years before they were needed. When they were finally able to join in the Christmas fun by holding up stockings for Rachel and Deidre, life was complete for all six little hooks. Their mission was clear, and they were up to the task. Each little brass hook loved her life's work. Of course, they did spend eleven months in hibernation, but that only made their little muscles all the stronger for the grand task of holding tight to their precious burden of stuffed Christmas Stockings.

After many, many years—nineteen to be exact—the six little Christmas Stocking hooks overheard a discussion that caught their attention. Just as they were waking from their hibernation, Grandma was heard to say that this year there should be a change: maybe it was time to retire some of the hooks. Grandpa agreed that since Dana was living so far away now, maybe Hook One's stocking should be mailed to her. Grandma added that Chelsea, who now had her own apartment, might like to have her stocking to hang in her own home. The last few years had brought changes in the family's Christmas holiday, and more changes were sure to occur. Desiree, who was grown up, would soon be out on her own, and Delia, Rachel and Deidre would follow.

And so it came to pass. Dana's and Chelsea's Christmas Stockings were mailed away. And though all six little hooks would still be twisted into the fireplace mantle shelf, only four would be occupied this Christmas, 2004.

Hooks One and Two were mellow with the unexpected lifting of their Christmas burden, because they had been loyal and faithful in fulfilling their task throughout the years. They would quietly watch the fun this year, knowing very well that their future would be filled with many more Christmas Stockings and many more children. The house was big and sturdy, and it would host many families in the future.

After Christmas 2004, Grandma removed the little hooks from their posts under the shelf and carefully stored them in their tight little box. She knew that although two of them would not be used for a while, it was only a temporary retirement. She reminded herself that when the house was sold, the little hooks would be given as a special gift to the new owners.

And, oh, what memories were stored in the hearts and minds of the six little girls. They had wonderful memories of all their growing years romping through the big house, strewing Christmas Stocking "stuff" wherever they ran. Grandpa's hooks and their precious burdens had become part of the fabric of the little girls' lives—for that matter, the whole family's lives—just as he had intended that long, long ago morning in 1985.

SALLY
AND
HARRY

Life is uncharted territory. It reveals its story one moment at a time.

—LEO BUSCAGLIA

Prologue

My home is near a forest, and there are many tall trees in my yard. I live with my Sally in a nest in the largest of all the trees. These are sacred ancestral grounds, and our nest has been the home of my ancestors for centuries. It consists of several pieces of ancient wood framed into sturdy branches with debris and dried leaves within for comfort. It's very strong and makes us feel secure. It also helps keep me connected to my ancestors.

Our tree stands in front of a large house where two very peculiar humans live. Sally and I have two hind legs and two front legs, and we use all of them to hold nuts or jump, run, climb trees and walk. The humans have only two legs; they don't jump, climb or even run; they just walk—slowly. As I said, they're peculiar. One of them is tall and slim and uses tools that clatter loudly and roar and blow like the wind. The other—a female I think—is short, round, quiet and gives us nuts. I don't trust them, but they've never done us any harm.

There are also two cats that live on the property. I don't like them at all. There's a black long-haired female cat that stays mostly in the house and a gray short-haired male cat that stays mostly outside. The gray cat doesn't appear to be interested in us, but I've seen what he does to birds, mice and lizards. He's really bad. Even though he pretends that he doesn't see us, I know he watches us closely. When he's near, I keep Sally close and bark at him loudly.

The humans like to keep in our good graces by giving us a type of nut that doesn't grow on our trees; their nuts are different, but they're quite good. The tall human fastened a bowl onto the railing of the back deck, and the short one fills it with nuts once a day. When the short one forgets to fill the bowl, I bark and rap the deck rail hard. That usually brings her running.

During the long, warm summer days, we like to lie in the sun. The deck rail is just the right width for us to stretch out our arms and legs. Even then, I keep a sharp lookout for the gray cat, so as to keep my Sally safe. It's my mission to always be on guard for her. I am her bodyguard, and I'm good at it.

Chapter One

I have early memories of many squirrels living in my neighborhood, ancients and youths alike. Back then the squirrels were all family and friends. My friends and I spent hours practicing to be fierce warriors, rescuing fair maidens from spoilers. We all dreamed regularly of performing splendid deeds of bravery.

For reasons I've never known, a year or so ago everyone disappeared, one-by-one. It must have been a mass migration and someone forgot to tell me. I was the only squirrel left. The whole experience was, and still is, a mystery. I was left behind with black crows, blue jays, woodpeckers and various small birds sharing my trees. Where had all my family and friends gone?

I continued practicing my warrior ways alone, wishing for fair maidens to rescue. But the joy was gone. What's the sense in practicing fair maiden rescues if there are no fair maidens to be rescued? It was such a lonely existence that I considered moving to another neighborhood, but that was before Sally.

Chapter Two

Last winter, after a long, lonely trek up and down my regular path of trees, I returned to my nest to find it had been visited. Nothing was missing, but my comfortable pile of leaves had been disturbed, and my body didn't fit quite right anymore.

My immediate reaction was to set up such a loud barking racket that the intruder would know to stay away. Then, when I started sniffing around, I began to suspect that it might be another squirrel. For a short while I wondered if a fair maiden might be in need of rescuing. I wondered if I should brush up on my warrior skills. But nightfall came quickly, and it was too late to start a thorough investigation, so I did my best to rest. Of course, I didn't sleep a wink.

Early the next morning, groggy as I was, I ran down my tree without stopping to run my toes through the birdbath, for I was anxious to start my search. I searched all the trees in front of the house with no luck. I ran across the roof of the house and clambered into my huge, ancient oak tree, thinking that a new squirrel might have settled in one of its huge branches. No luck. So I ran to the trees next door.

Traveling into and across the yard next door can be a terrifying experience because there are a couple of huge, hairy, scary dogs that have to be carefully watched. Usually I sit on the top of the fence and look all around before venturing into their area. This time I was in such a dither to find a new squirrel that I was careless and jumped off the fence, almost landing on one of the dogs. Luckily it was the older of the two, and he had a hard time running. It was a warning to me, though, that I should be more careful. Those dogs bark and slobber and drag their toys all over their yard; they jump around so carelessly that if one of them had caught and used me as a toy, I would have been full of holes within minutes.

Sobered and chastened, I continued my search. I dashed across the street watching carefully for the cars that occasionally drove by. I found not even a hint of the stranger. I ventured into the forest for a small distance, but decided it was too dangerous to go further. There are animals in the forest that I don't like to think about. In my youth, my ancestors taught me many lessons of the horrors in the forest.

I spent the next week wandering and searching my neighborhood for the strange squirrel with no results. I decided that my loneliness had played tricks on me. There was no one in or near my neighborhood, or I would have found him, for I was very thorough in my search.

I decided to spend one last morning searching and then quit wasting my time and energy on a non-happening. Early in the afternoon, tired and disheartened, I returned home. I was so depressed that, for the second time in one week, I was careless, running straight up to my nest without watching for humans, dogs or cats. Once there, to my astonishment, I found a very sleepy, frightened and beautiful fair maiden curled in my nest.

Chapter Three

In all my wandering and searching, I never imagined such a lovely vision. I didn't know such a creature existed; she didn't look real. I felt like I was struck by lightning, and I instantly fell under her spell.

It took me several hours to calm her so that she could tell me about herself. The adventures she told were terrifying—almost as frightening as the stories my ancestors told when I was small. She had been lost for weeks in the forest and like my ancestors, she described animals that I could only imagine.

She completed her tale by telling me that she had watched me from the upper branches of my tree for several weeks. When I left in the morning, she dropped into my nest to sleep until late afternoon when she knew I would return. Then she would climb to an upper branch and watch me through the night.

I desperately searched through my memory of the last couple of weeks to recall how many of my foolish posturings as a savior of fair maidens she might have seen. I knew my secret was safe, though, when she told me that she knew I could be trusted.

Chapter Four

Her name is Sally. By the way, did I tell you that my name is Harry? With the introduction of Sally into my life, my whole world changed. I now had a companion, and the enormity of my new responsibilities was almost staggering. Now that I had this priceless beauty in my life, and in my heart, I had to be a real bodyguard. I had to grow; I had to be worthy. I realized this in a paralyzing moment of clarity that changed my whole world.

I now had my very own fair maiden. As her bodyguard, I had to discipline myself. The fact that she was able to make her way into my tree and sleep in my nest without my knowledge was a real wakeup call. I had to do better; I now had someone to care for, and I had to be fierce in my assignment. She had to be perfectly safe in my care.

From that day forward, I scoped the neighborhood carefully before Sally ventured out of our nest. I barked ferociously so that any intruder would know that I was armed and able. I scaled each fence and examined each tree. I guarded her fiercely.

While I guarded, Sally became skilled at locating and carrying home bits of materials that were perfect for enlarging our nest. Her ideas modernized our nest and made it more comfortable. I was proud. Sally and I embarked on our new life together.

My days were altered and much more interesting. Sally looks at the world from a totally different view. For instance, I don't trust the people that live in the house beneath our nest. Sally likes them, and if I don't guard her carefully against it, she would play with them. She has a mind of her own, though, which makes it difficult to keep her safe.

We both enjoy sunbathing on the railing of the back deck. One afternoon as the tall human was laying on his back in the sun, Sally ran down the tree, onto the rail, onto the deck and leaped onto his stomach. For a split second, she sat looking straight into his eyes. The human was so surprised that he just lay there looking at her. When she leaped off, he jumped up laughing and yelling. Sally's so fearless that she worries me. I try and try to make her aware of the dangers, but she just goes her own way, making life difficult for her bodyguard.

I've watched the humans and know their habits, so when they're home and the bowl is empty, I sit on the deck rail near the empty bowl until they notice that I'm waiting. I try to keep Sally in the upper branches while I watch for the humans. She won't sit quietly, though. She raps the tree branches loudly and barks to let them know we're there and we're hungry. When the door opens and the human comes out, I want to run up into the top branches too, but I can't—Sally must be protected! I try to keep Sally above and behind me, but too often, down she leaps, waiting only a short distance from the door, until the human goes back into the house. It takes every ounce of my bravery to keep ahead of my Sally; I have to stay razor sharp as her bodyguard.

Chapter Five

One of the things about Sally that I love is her calm disposition. However, during early spring of this year, Sally became a bit quarrelsome. Since it was unusual for her to be irritable, I decided that I would take a few extra tours around the neighborhood each afternoon, just to stay out of old Sally's way. After a week of extra afternoon tours, I returned home to quite a surprise. Sally was sitting with a big grin on her face, and there were three squirmy, tiny lumps lying in our nest. On close inspection, I saw that they were baby squirrels! To my astonishment, she said they were ours and that we were now a family of five. Who knew?

But that was only the beginning. Baby squirrels take a lot of time. And since I don't do baby squirrels, I made it clear to her that I wasn't going to give that time. Considering Sally's temperament of late, I expected a rough response. To my surprise, Sally remained jolly. All she wanted from me was protection for the nest and her little squirrels, which I was happy to provide; after all, I am her bodyguard. And, of course, I brought things for her to eat. She refused to leave those little squirrels even to find acorns.

When the three babies were asleep, Sally occasionally ran up and down the tree trunk a bit, but other than that, she was insistent on sitting in the nest watching over them. She watched me intently. I got the feeling that she expected me to harm her little squirrels. That hurt my feelings. She shouldn't have worried—I didn't want to hurt them, I only wanted them to move out of our nest. I wanted my Sally back. I wanted my companion back. I was lonely.

Chapter Six

After about two months, the little intruders began imitating our chatter. It was funny. Then they started trying to climb out of the nest. I was very happy about that. Sally was content to have them moving around, so I decided that maybe I could help in their migration to another area—the further away the better.

I showed them how to jump from one branch to another. It's hard to explain how hardheaded they were. They wouldn't listen. They insisted on jumping onto any branch within reach. They wouldn't think. I told them over and over that a small branch would bend and drop under their weight. I thought they'd never learn to jump only onto strong branches. For a few weeks, our old oak tree's branches were always swinging up and down under the weight of the little numbskulls. But gradually, one by one, they learned.

I was exhausted from all the jumping lessons, so I decided to let Sally take over the rest of their education. She loved it. Day after day she was out in the trees teaching those squirrels about dogs, cats, food, wind, scents, insects, owls and all the other important lessons of life. Sally was a good teacher.

To my surprise, though, I found myself watching and listening ever closer as the days went by. I found myself wanting to help in those lessons of life that I knew so well. I listened to Sally teach them about life while she took them on "nature walks" around our neighborhood. Nature walks indeed! Those little squirrels needed to be taught about Snake Rock, the forest and dastardly dogs. They needed to be prepared for the world by me.

I wanted those little squirrels properly prepared to face life out there in the wild. And, most surprising of all, I actually wanted to be with them; I liked them. I was lonely without the noisy little pests constantly chattering at me. So I went back to helping Sally with their lessons. I was pleased that Sally was beginning to trust me with them.

I took the little guys far and wide across our neighborhood and, of course, into the forest. Learning about the forest was a very important lesson. Sally was petrified of it and had no desire to ever enter into those shadowy areas again. But forest lessons were necessary to harden the little guys. I taught them the ways of the world, and my Sally was grateful. We were a team again.

Chapter Seven

A most important lesson for the three young ones was that they had to learn to be vigilant around Snake Rock. They feared nothing, and I knew it was vitally important for them to learn about the area of the Rock. Snake Rock was behind our property in a spot deeply shaded by old oak trees and tall, bushy shrubs. Before my ancestors disappeared, they had taught me that all of the area around Snake Rock was bad adventure territory. Snake Rock was home for many snakes. Old snake skins and dried rattles were thickly scattered all around the area. Snake Rock had a bad aura.

But do you think I could get those little dunces to listen to me? On an average of once a week, I had to yank one of the three back from wandering into the area. They had no fear. One afternoon when I was out looking for them, I spotted a snake on its way to "visit" with the little guys. All three were sitting within the risky area when I found them and saw the slithering danger. I made a huge commotion. I barked, chattered, leaped around and carried on something ferocious, which made the snake disappear. I felt quite heroic. And all three were properly impressed with my bravery. They ran home to Sally with tales of a wild rescue. Hearing them brag about me brought back memories of lonelier days, when I spent much of my time imagining feats of daring-do.

Life was exciting again. The little ones learned well, and I was proud of all their accomplishments. I was very surprised when I realized that their progress made me as happy as it did my Sally. The little guys were important to me.

Chapter Eight

Early one morning I woke to find that everyone was up and gone. No one had mentioned special plans for the day. I puzzled around the nest for a while, before becoming just a bit alarmed. The hairs on the back of my neck were just beginning to stand, when I heard a distant sound that sent me running down our tree to look for Sally and my guys. I hit the ground running, listening hard to get a fix on the frightened sounds. My family was in distress. My bodyguard instincts immediately took over.

At last, I found all of my family. Sally and two of our little sons were safe, but the third had managed to get himself caught in a chain link fence. His head was stuck tight, and he couldn't get free. He was frightened, but quiet, just as he had been taught: stay calm and don't panic. That was one of his first lessons.

I quickly quieted Sally; she knew I could save our little squirrel. It made me proud to know that she trusted me. But my son was in real trouble! I had to think fast! There had to be a way to get him out of that fence before those dastardly dogs became aware.

Luckily our son had climbed nearly to the top before he got stuck. A plan that might work quickly occurred to me. Our son was going to have a very sore neck, but I saw no other way to free him. While warning Sally that there might be some blood, I leaped onto the tree nearest our endangered son. I called my other two sons to follow. They followed. I gave them the strategy, and like little soldiers, without hesitation, they followed onto the branch nearest the fence, and from the trunk of the tree out toward its tip.

The branch dropped slowly as we moved outward. Under our combined weight, the branch dropped right to the edge of the fence. I could almost touch the top of my trapped son's little head. My calculations had been right. My sons lined up behind me and we held tight to the branch with our claws. I warned all three that this was going to hurt all of us, but it had to be done. We all knew the plan and we were prepared for the pain. I firmly clamped my teeth onto my trapped son's tail. As instructed, the little guy directly behind me clamped onto my tail with his teeth, and the last one did the same on his brother's tail. Then, with our claws solidly clasped around the tree branch, we slowly inched backward, clasping and unclasping our claws as we inched back toward the trunk of the tree. The pain in our tails was immense, but not one of us let go.

Slowly, ever so slowly, as we pulled with all our strength, the little head inched out of its trap. My sons were so brave and quiet that I almost burst with pride. Then, with a soft "pop" and a squeak, his little head pulled free. At the same time, all three of us let go of the branch and our assigned tails. All four of us dropped to the ground. To my horror, I saw a huge dog bearing down on us with saliva flying from his mouth and a mad gleam in his eyes. We had dropped on the wrong side of the fence, and Sally was sitting precisely where we had dropped.

This was real trouble, because I had the three little ones and Sally to corral and protect. She was terrified. I instantly shouted instructions to my two heroic sons to grab their mother and run. At the same time I pushed my rescued son as hard as I could and told him to run, run faster than he knew he could. Just as the vicious animal roared over me, I leaped up and jabbed his face with a right hook. It didn't even faze him. I leaped up again and clawed his nose, while chattering and barking loudly. It confused him, but he didn't stop. In the background I could hear Sally trying to keep our sons from coming to my aid. I didn't want their help. This was my fight.

I could smell and feel dog breath. With my last ounce of strength, I made one final leap, landing on top of his head. I held on tight as he swung around crazed, trying to throw me. When he threw himself onto his side, I leaped off his head and dashed for the fence. I vaulted over the fence, landing safely on the ground right at Sally's feet. She hugged me over and over again while our sons chattered all around our feet. The dog was slobbering and barking on the other side of the fence.

Sally scolded all three boys, pointing out the danger we all faced because of the carelessness of one of them. She told them over and over again how lucky they were to have a hero for a Dad. I had to tell her to stop because I was embarrassed. My chest swelled with pride at her words, but most of all I was so pleased at how well my sons had learned this most important lesson: when one was in trouble, the other two were right at my side to help.

That night, after we were safely snuggled in our nest, I told all three of them how proud I was to be their Dad. It took weeks for all of our tails to heal properly.

Chapter Nine

Gradually they started leaving home without us and staying away longer and longer. Even though I no longer worried about their ability to survive out in the world, I was concerned that they might build their nests in another neighborhood far away. I wanted to build their nests now, in our family tree, sort of as an inducement for them to return. Surprisingly, Sally wasn't a bit worried. She seemed to know it was time for our sons to leave. Sally said I had to let them go, that they would know when it was time to return. She told me how proud she was of me, that I had taught them the lessons they needed in order to make their way in the world. She was serene and comfortably resigned with their leaving, but it made me crazy.

Our sons foraged further and further from home until one day, one of them failed to return. By the time fall arrived, there were no more young squirrels in our nest, just my Sally and me. Home alone. It wasn't easy. The night the first one failed to come home, Sally had to block my way to keep me from storming down the tree trunk to find him. She informed me that he had gone courting. I didn't even know what courting was. If you will remember, my youth had been cut short by the great migration of all my family and friends, and I was totally alone until Sally came along.

The next morning, my son came in with a surprise. He was leading a pretty little squirrel along by her paw, and she was so cute that I thought immediately of my Sally when I first found her. My son told me that there was a huge branch just above our nest, and he wanted to build a nest for her. Sally had said he'd be back—she was right—how did she know these things?

I was so excited that I started to dismantle part of our nest so that we could build a good solid nest for our son using some of my ancestors' remnants. Sally had to stop me, cautioning that there were two more sons and we had to save enough ancestral remnants for all of their nests. Of course she was right. And how did she know they would all be back? Some things mystify me. We built a sturdy nest on the branch just above ours, and I kept my eye on the kids. It's hard for a bodyguard to know when his job is finished.

Epilogue

Life has become sweet again. Sally and I are back to our life of running up and down tree trunks, rummaging around our neighborhood looking for acorns to eat, and sunning on the deck rail. We now have a great deal of visiting to do also. There are many more squirrels in our neighborhood. I've come through the harrowing experience of raising a family. I'm older, and I have much wisdom to share with the younger squirrels. I don't know where the time went, but I'm now an ancestor.

My life is more relaxed, too. After watching over a bunch of wild little squirrels, being a bodyguard for only my Sally is a snap.

Now that winter has come, all three young ones are in their own sturdy nests in our big tree, each built with bits of my ancestral remnants. And I now have seven squirrels to love and to worry over, as my family has extended to include my Sally, three sons and three new daughters-in-law. I think of my lonely struggle after the great migration. I think of finding my Sally and the hard work of raising a family of three. I'm proud of the job we've done.

One recent stormy evening while Sally and I were snuggled in our nest, I whispered to her how happy I was that we did such a good job. I told her that raising a family was such a hard task that it was a good thing we only had to do it once. Now we could spend the rest of our lives peacefully.

Sally rose up, crinkled her eyes at me and informed me that in the spring we would start all over again. I don't remember what happened next. Could I have passed out? I remember Sally fanning me with a piece of cardboard. "Sally, can we just do one this time? Maybe you could even find us a little girl? Boys are too hard."

And life goes on.

MR. McELHANEY

I think that I shall never roam in gardens where one finds a gnome.

—WANNA NEWMAN

Chapter One

Mr. McElhaney explodes, "I want this ended now! I won't have it! It's hard I've worked for my coin! It's meant for my old years! I demand that this stop!"

Mr. McElhaney was having a furious fit. "I don't know who's behind it but I want the eejit sheriff called, now!"

Mr. McElhaney stomped around in a circle muttering aloud with an occasional outburst of language so vile that even he was ashamed of himself. But he had worked himself into such a state that he couldn't stop. This was dire. He needed help to control … all of a sudden Mr. McElhaney stopped his frenzy. He leaped forward and dropped to the ground. Under a mound of withered leaves, under a rose bush, he had spotted something. A furious "aha" burst from him and he scrabbled under the leaves, furiously pushing them aside to pick up a small cloth bag secured by a yellow ribbon. It held something heavy, and Mr. McElhaney knew exactly what it was and exactly how many there were in the bag and just exactly how much they were worth.

Mr. McElhaney poured four shiny quarters from the small bag into his outspread hand. Yes, the quarters were his. Mr. McElhaney knew each and every coin that belonged to him. But he hadn't put his bag of precious coin under that mound of leaves. This treachery must stop.

Chapter Two

Within the house a somewhat elderly woman was looking out the window watching the goings on of the little gnome who lived nestled within her roses. It was unusual for him to be so active during the daytime; he was a nocturnal creature. She had no sympathy for the gnome, for she knew just exactly how stingy he was. She also had strong suspicions as to his method of gathering "his" coin.

Mr. McElhaney was a petty thief. He thought no one was wise to his nightly jaunts around the neighborhood, but she knew. She knew how he crept off after dark and scoured the nearby streets, driveways and porches for fallen change. This type of coin gathering didn't bother her, but she worried that he also slipped into unlocked autos and scrounged around their floors and seats. She worried that he might even peer into the glove compartment for anything that might jingle in his hands.

There were times when coins were missing from her dresser top. There had never been anything of real value missing, so the woman hadn't felt the need for chastising. It was her belief that some people, Mr. McElhaney being one such, were just meant to be on the far side of society and nothing was going to change his ways. So she just watched carefully to see that no serious harm came from his petty thievery.

Chapter Three

The man of the house had kept his own counsel for a good long time. He hadn't liked any of the goings on but had decided to bide his time.

Sure enough, in time, an idea came to him. Mr. McElhaney needed to have his comeuppance; a grand idea, indeed.

Granddaughters had begun to make their way into his life, his home and his heart. They were little girls who loved his stories; greedy little girls who loved jingling coins. And they loved Grandpa and Grandma, who could always be counted on to give them something to take home in their little pockets after a visit. It was the perfect foil to Mr. McElhaney's thieving ways.

Chapter Four

Mr. McElhaney became the source of another wonderful grandpa story. The six little girls were made aware of his nightly roaming. Grandpa's stories told of Mr. McElhaney's probable thievery, that he was a miser, he was nasty tempered, and he would bite and spit if he ever caught anyone handling his coin. Grandpa explained that the little girls should seek out his fortune quietly and immediately run away if he looked at them. Maybe, just maybe, if they ever found a small cloth bag, it might be snatched out from under his hiding place safely.

Mr. McElhaney was after all, a gnome—an Irish gnome at that—and everyone knows that gnomes only roam at night. The granddaughters were assured that if they snatched his fortune bags during the day, they should be safe. The cranky little gnome slept soundly all day long because his nights were filled with nefarious activities.

Chapter Five

Grandpa told his story well and his little granddaughters were charmed with the idea of turning Mr. McElhaney upside down. Year after year, when the little girls came to visit, the very first thing they did when they tumbled from their various family vehicles was to start their hunt for Mr. McElhaney's treasure. Since everyone knows gnomes sleep with one eye open, sometimes it took hours to find his treasure because they had to appear blasé in their hunting. Mr. McElhaney must not be made aware of their true mission.

Chapter Six

Every Christmas Eve, every Easter, every Mother's Day and Father's Day; in other words, every visit to Grandpa's and Grandma's house started the same way. The little girls looked high and low, mostly low, for Mr. McElhaney's coin. Since he didn't know when they were coming, it was a certainty that he would lose some coin to them. The granddaughters were often curious that they could find only one bag of coin. However, Mr. McElhaney was no dummy. It took only a few holiday visits for him to realize the girls were going to rip him off, and he soon charted his actions. As soon as daylight fell on the first evening of their arrival, Mr. McElhaney frantically made sure the rest of his treasure was hidden very well.

However, gnomes become careless just like humans. Therefore, over the weeks and months between visits he was always shocked when the hordes of small female humans descended on him. He lost many bags of his treasure to the nimble, flitting little girls.

Chapter Seven

A number of years passed with many bags hidden and many bags located. By the time of Mr. McElhaney's final conniption fit and his demand for help from the "eejit sheriff," the little girls were not so little anymore. If truth be told, the granddaughters were just humoring old Grandpa with his game. They would much rather sit off by themselves in a cluster and talk about … well … whatever cousins talk about when they gather at their grandparents' house.

Chapter Eight

After many years, on another sunny summer day, Mr. McElhaney threw another fit, but this time, he was met with the hilarious giggles of three preteens and three teenagers. They thought the whole thing was outrageously funny and told him so, saying, "Would you please sit down, stop this silliness, look at your ridiculous behavior, and you should be ashamed of yourself."

Mr. McElhaney hasn't moved a muscle since that day, at least not when any human could see him. But he hasn't lost any bags of coin either. The little granddaughters have outgrown him.

Chapter Nine

It might interest those six little granddaughters to know why Mr. McElhaney was such a thieving little gnome. And by the way, he didn't look on it as thievery. Any coin left on the ground, on the floor of an unlocked car, or even on the top of a table or dresser was fair game to anyone who came along. He would never have gone through glove compartments. Mr. McElhaney knew right from wrong. He was a lawful fellow. It hurt his feelings when he heard Grandpa's stories of his supposed thievery. If Mr. McElhaney's coin had been out in the open, it would have served him right to have the little girls rip him off. But it was downright naughty of them to look under leaves and overturn pots to swipe his beautiful bags right out from under him. Wrong, wrong, wrong. No wonder he turned into a cranky, spiteful being. Mr. McElhaney felt very misunderstood.

Chapter Ten

As tranquil as Mr. McElhaney's life was, the advent of the little girls plunged him into a quandary. He knew as well as he knew his age, weight and height that any object lying out in the open was his for the taking. But his nights were sleepless as he lay wondering about the coin that he found inside the automobiles that were carelessly left unlocked. He had been raised knowing that if it was available to him, it was fair game. But when the little girls started stealing his bags of coin, he had to confront his own behavior and conform it to his unhappiness with their behavior. If he took coin from humans, even careless humans, then how could he become so enraged when the little girls stole away his bags of coin? It was a dilemma.

Chapter Eleven

However, Mr. McElhaney was a gnome, and gnomes are generally very sure of themselves. So, it was only natural for him to confront his problem and resolve it within a short period. In actuality, he didn't lose much sleep. He was right, and they were wrong. But the little girls could be forgiven because they were human and they were small. He had a hard time admitting it to himself, but they were really loveable. And they enjoyed their thievery almost as much as he enjoyed his. It should be pointed out, though, his was not thievery: he was building his fortune for his old years.

THE
SCENT
OF
LILACS

When lilacs last in the dooryard bloomed
And the great star early drooped in the western sky in the
night,
I mourned, and yet shall mourn with ever-returning spring.
Ever-returning spring, trinity sure to me you bring,
Lilac blooming perennial and drooping star in the west,
And thought of her I love.

—WALT WHITMAN

Chapter One

In Mr. McElhaney's dreams, he could actually smell the rich loam of his homeland, and he could see the acres of heather growing wild near the ancient bogs filled with peat. He could hear the wild roaring of the seas below the dangerous cliffs nearby.

However, he always waked quite content to be in his very own rose garden in America, where life was easy. His peaceful life consisted of daily slumbering during spring, summer and fall. A severe winter could be troublesome, but he always had piles of leaves around his feet that made good shelter from the wind, snow and rain. Like all gnomes, Mr. McElhaney had thick gnome skin, and the elements gave him only slight discomfort. His nights were busy with scurrying throughout his mountain neighborhood collecting coin. He found coin in crevices, under automobiles, on porches, near garage doors and twinkling at him under street lights. Humans were very careless about their coin, but Mr. McElhaney wasn't, for he had a long old age to worry about. He needed a huge fortune. He would live to an old, old age. He worked hard preparing for that old, old age, and life was good.

Chapter Two

When the lilacs bloomed, though, Mr. McElhaney had no control over reveries of his youth. When the lilacs bloomed, his visions were of a beautiful young female whose grace was unworldly. Her movements were unlike anything ever before seen. Her short, dark hair shone like spun glass. Her skin was pale perfection and . . . this was where Mr. McElhaney shook himself awake. That was then, this is now. Enough. But when a rustling breeze disturbed the lilacs, off he went, back into his dreamy state.

Chapter Three

Ireland was far away. His family had always been woodland gnomes, and as far back as memory went, Ireland had been their home. Gnomes were free to roam and make their lives as rich as their own particular talents would allow, like his new world in America. He had grown up dreaming to live, work and grow old in Ireland. But dreams do get blown away.

Chapter Four

Trolls are nasty creatures. Gnomes don't have anything to do with trolls. It usually isn't difficult to avoid them because trolls are rare in Ireland, but when Mr. McElhaney came across the wondrous creature of his dreams as a youth, he was in for an education.

Chapter Five

He glimpsed her across a crowded area. She took his breath away. He felt like he had been punched in the chest. Needless to say, he spent the next several days trying to find out who she was and where she lived. It took some doing because no one knew of a gnome who looked like his description of her. After questioning and badgering everyone who came into his path, he found out her name: Horatio. But to his horror, he was told that she was a troll.

Chapter Six

That made no sense. Everyone knew trolls were ugly and nasty. But Horatio was lovely. She could not be a troll. Someone made a mistake.

Chapter Seven

Horatio lived in a troll village, she had troll parents, and she had troll siblings. There was no mistake—Horatio was a troll. Now what?

Chapter Eight

No matter how hard Mr. McElhaney tried, he could not get Horatio to pay him any attention. She was happy in her troll world, and she had no time for a love-sick gnome. Still, he followed her. He dreamed about her. He tried to convince her that she was a gnome, but she laughed so hard that it hurt his feelings. He offered her the world (his gnome world), all to no avail. She had eyes only for other trolls.

Chapter Nine

Gnomes are meant to be happy, and they waste little time with "if only." There was just one thing Mr. McElhaney could do. He packed up his bag, left his beloved Ireland and set out for another land. After many years of travel and toil, he came to the heavenly land of Pine Valley, California. He made it his home and found a rose bed to his liking, and there he spends his busy days and nights building his fortune for his old years.

NOW YOU KNOW THE REST OF THE STORY!

A TEENY TINY STORY

Written for
Rachel Carly

You throw my ball and pat my head and let me in and out.
You keep me stocked with toys to chew and treats I'm wild
about.

—UNKNOWN

An Unresolved Problem

I live in some way cool digs with my family. Rachel is my favorite person in the whole world. She plays with me almost whenever I want, and she keeps me from being lonely. I have a play yard with interesting smells in every corner, and I have some cats that are sort of dipsticks. I mean, like, I'm almost totally happy.

I have one difficult problem. My right front paw ITCHES. My days are filled with trying to ease the scratchy ITCH. Even if I run around and around my house and yard, even if I jump on everything in my path (and get scolded), even if I bark at every sound I hear (and get scolded), it still ITCHES something awful. Did I mention that I'm an Australian Shepherd? Yes, I am, but don't call me Mate—you can, however, call me Dude. Actually my name is Ella Bella Stella or Elly Belly or just plain Ella.

My Rachel tells me that I can't dig in the yard but, like, digging is way cool and it's the only thing that soothes my paw ITCH. Our soil is wonderfully dirty interesting dirt. I try and try to forget the ITCH, and sometimes I'm sort of successful for a little while, but the minute the door opens and I get out into the open air, there it goes again—the ITCH, and I like, totally forget everything Rachel has dropped on me about digging. It's a woeful problem.

When I sit and reflect on my life, I realize how far I've come in recent months and just exactly how much I've learned. When I was a puppy I would, like, Hello?, make a puddle whenever I had an urge. Now I'm schooled; I've learned to hold it until I'm outside. That was quite an accomplishment. And I used to chew everything in sight, especially socks and shoes, which feel particularly good on my gums and teeth. But I learned that Rachel really, really doesn't like my chewing, so I gave it up (well, I've almost stopped chewing; sometimes I slip, but I hide my chews now). I still have a hard time not jumping up onto the furniture because that's where some totally good smells are and, like, it's very comfortable up there.

One of life's mysteries is that my Rachel can jump on the furniture and I can't, but so be it: I stay on the floor just for her. And I just totally love to jump on people, especially when I see someone new. I don't know why this is not a good thing, because I can tell by the looks on their faces that people enjoy it, but Rachel bags on me about it and sternly says, "Down," so I have almost stopped doing this. Not completely, because I get excited, but almost. I understand "roll," "up," "leave it," "take it," and "stay." I'm quite advanced in my obedience lessons.

When I look back on my accomplishments, I'm proud of myself. I sit when Rachel tells me to sit, I come when she tells me to come (almost always anyway), and I fetch for her. These were all, like, totally hard things to learn. I've really developed a lot of discipline just for my Rachel. But my paw still ITCHES and the only thing that eases my ITCH is to dig in some cool, damp, really dirty dirt, which gets Rachel totally upset. Wonder why?

My cats are no help at all because they won't dig except in one particular box, and like, duh, how dumb is that? I'm clueless as to the fun in that; they just scratch a little bit and then leave. And speaking of my cats, I have three. Six is a real turkey—that cat doesn't like me at all! Speck is okay, he's cool, but Toulouse is way cool—he's my bud, like: "Yo, what's up?" and he's ready to hang out.

Toulouse tries to help with my ITCH, but he doesn't have any real understanding of my love for dirt. He won't even get his nose dirty; when I tell him to stick his nose in the dirt, he says, "No way," and I tell him, "Yes way." But he won't, and he really, really doesn't like to get his paws dirty. Funny! He'll sit and watch and sometimes he'll jump into my digging spot, just for fun.

But he doesn't have the ITCH, so how could he really get with it?

Could I drop some knowledge on Rachel about digging in the dirt? Maybe if I could figure out a way to make Rachel's right front paw ITCH then I could show her how digging soothes the ITCH. Would that help her understand that digging is a therapy, not disobedience?

I MUST PONDER THIS PROBLEM ...

WE SAID—SHE SAID

The rule for today:
Touch my tail, I shred your hand.
New rule tomorrow.

—UNKNOWN

Chapter One

We Said

Our cast of characters is varied, but we think you will agree that the most unique character is Two Boots, or Boots, or Bootie, or Boo. Take your pick.

The first six months of its life are a mystery, it having been dropped onto our laps at about that age. When we first came across the cat, it was a sorry mess. Someone had left it in an office building garage, tied with a rope to a pair of ragged trousers. The rope, the trousers and the cat were tangled into a snarly knot. There was a small amount of dry cat food nearby, but no water. The cat lay in a lump and didn't move, barely alive. We picked it up and held it. It just sagged in our arms.

It was very curious in appearance. It was black, with a little white here and there. It had excessively short legs and a body like a tube—a long, hairy tube. We felt sorry for it. That was our first mistake. We took it home with us. That was our second mistake. Much later, we were told of the "Munchkin" cat. A Munchkin can be compared to the Dachshund with its long body and short legs.

With an infusion of expensive, healthy cat food, plenty of fresh water and a warm, loving home, it quickly gained strength and health. All went reasonably well for the first couple of weeks. It ran around the house sniffing everything and sticking its claws into every crevice it could reach. And it climbed, oh, did it climb! And it jumped in ecstasy when the front door opened, dashing outside to smell all the new outside scents. Its little back would arch into a hump, and it would leap sideways with the sheer joy of being alive. We were delighted. We thought we were so lucky to have found this little creature.

However, there were problems. Our first hint came when our really good cat (a big white fluffy cat) chose to leave home rather than live with it. We fought that problem by begging, pleading and groveling for several weeks, until we finally convinced the good cat to come back home. We thought we could relax. Nope.

The claw problem came next: we discovered after a careful inspection that our two suede chairs needed protection immediately! We also had the spay problem: we discovered it was a she and that she needed attention immediately! When the two problems were taken care of—with some expense, and her toes and tummy incision had properly healed, again we thought we could relax. Nope.

She developed a neurosis. After two months of living with us and visiting with all our family and friends in a perfectly normal way, she decided she was afraid of them—all of them. She also decided that biting was very satisfying — biting everyone. It was at this point that she decided she preferred hiding under our bed, to being gracious with our family and friends.

And, because of her odd obsession with the space under our bed, if she hears a strange voice, she heads for the bed. When she hears a strange car come into our driveway, under the bed she goes. When the doorbell rings, under the bed she goes. There have even been times when the ringing of the telephone sends her under the bed. Boots is peculiar.

And now, because of her persistence in biting, we must always approach her with caution. If we pet her, we must be on guard about her tail—don't touch it—she bites. And don't touch her tummy—she bites. She likes us to scratch her ears, but when we stop—she bites. Actually, when we stop scratching anything on her—she bites. When her food isn't placed exactly where she wants—she bites. When our good cat returned, deciding that she could, after all, live with Boots, Boots stayed in a constant attack mode. Boots is vicious.

Her biting is a real problem. When we leave home, we have red bite marks all over our hands, arms and legs. In the morning, we try very hard to please her with a brushing session. We were given a magic brush by a barber named Ben. It works wonders with Boots' fur. The Ben Brush is round and has short rubber prongs forming a circle. She loves that brush. We brush and brush until we're so tired that we have to stop. But if she isn't satisfied with our efforts (and she rarely is), yep—she bites. Sometimes we have to shove her out the door and shut it quickly to keep from having our ankles bitten. We may already have told you about this, but it's so disconcerting that it should be mentioned twice.

We actually thought when our grandchildren came to stay with us for a short while that Boots would become accustomed to them. We thought she would come out from under the bed and help entertain them. That didn't happen. Instead, in order to keep her from starving herself to death, we had to feed her under the bed. Boots is strange.

She Said

Keep in mind that there are two sides to every story. With that said, I'm not peculiar, I'm not vicious and I'm not strange. However, I am unique. Much of my time is spent dealing with the many humans I come into contact with. Because of the malevolent nature of many of these humans, I spend a lot of time under the bed.

The first months of my life are a mystery to me, but I have always had a strange urge to curl up under things. I especially like to sleep under newspapers. One thing I don't like, though, is trouser legs—men's trouser legs in particular. They sort of make me feel like I can't breathe. Curious, but there it is. And I don't like rope!

What I do remember is that a long time ago, two people picked me up very carefully and stroked my fur gently. For a short time, I thought maybe they were my mother and father.

They carried me to a warm house and gave me such a huge amount of good food that it upset my digestive system, but my body learned to love it, and I grew very fast.

When I first came to live in my house, a huge white cat lurked around, watching me. Because it left the day after I moved in, it took me several weeks to get to know that old cat. It must have had plans that couldn't be changed. But it came back after a while, and we got along pretty well after that, sort of.

By the way, I have long, shiny, black fur. I have lovely white fur under my chin; one might say a fur bib. I have extraordinary white and black coloring on my tummy, all blended together in a most unusual way. I have gorgeous knee-high, white fur boots (get it—I'm Boots?) on my hind legs, and delicate white scalloped socks on my front feet. I have a white muzzle with a black smudge on my pretty pink nose. My body is extremely long and I have short legs. I'm beautiful.

In my home I can run, climb and scratch—well, I used to be able to scratch. There are two chairs in my living room made of wonderfully strong stuff, and I used to be able to scratch them and pretend that I was fighting them. I always won. Scratching those chairs made my toes feel good.

After I had been in my new home for a few weeks, I woke up with something dreadfully wrong. I meowed and screeched at the top of my lungs. I roamed aimlessly around the house until they picked me up, stuffed me into the travel box and took me for a ride to a pet hospital.

Things changed after that trip. I don't really know what happened. I thought we were going for a ride to soothe me because of my uncontrollable screeching. But when we arrived at our destination (I learned later it was the dreaded pet hospital), someone stuck something sharp in my side, and I went to sleep. When I woke up, my tummy hurt, my front feet hurt and I had a headache.

By the time my people came and took me home, I had formed two strong suspicions: my people probably weren't my parents, and humans aren't always nice. They aren't to be trusted.

Now I watch my people very carefully, and if I think they're going to sling me into the travel box, I dash for safety. That's right—under the bed. When I hear a strange voice outside my window, it could be someone who wants to touch me and scratch me in all the wrong places, so—under the bed. When a car comes into my driveway, it could be someone to take me back to that pet hospital, so—under the bed. When I hear the doorbell, it could be a visitor who will stay for days and throw my whole life into chaos, so, once again—under the bed. When I hear the telephone, I know it could mean a disruption to my schedule, so, of course—under the bed. Do you blame me for being super careful?

And something happened to my front claws when I went to the pet hospital. They used to be right at the tips of my front toes. Now I can't find them. They were useful because I could scratch with them—myself or others. Now, I no longer have them to protect myself from obnoxious humans or dangerous animals. Scratching and petting are harmless, and most humans seem to enjoy my fur. So, if someone wants to sit with me in a peaceful manner with their hands leisurely stroking my fur, that's fine, I'll allow it. But when they touch my tail, that's it—I bite. And they better not touch my tummy! If someone scratches behind my ears, or under my chin, that's fine, I allow it. But I don't want the scratching to stop until I've had enough because that upsets me, and, yes—I'll bite.

And I don't know why brushing me is such a chore for my people. I only get brushed twice a day, in the morning, if I'm quick enough to catch them before they leave, and at night, if I beg long enough. Can you blame me for showing irritation when they stop? Of course not—so I bite.

And about my food being in the wrong place, what's so hard about putting my food in the same spot twice a day? Anyone with common sense knows my food should be placed just exactly two inches from my water bowl. If it isn't there, I'll bite. What's the big deal about a little biting anyway? Their skin heals quickly.

And I don't give a fig who thinks that big white cat was "the really good cat!"—I know better. It used to walk by me and say bad things. I couldn't hear exactly what it was saying, but it frightened me—so I bit. Of course I couldn't bite her; she was bigger than me, so I bit the nearest human. Anyway, she left for good one day, and now I'm the only cat. Well, the only cat living in the house, anyway. There is another cat, Norman, but thank goodness he lives in the garage.

Did you ever have six people just drop in and not leave for two months? Well, I did. One Monday evening the doorbell rang. So I dashed under the bed to wait it out. Those people didn't leave Tuesday or Wednesday or Thursday or Friday or Saturday or Sunday. By the next Monday, I knew I was in for a long siege. My food and water were finally placed near the bed, so at least I didn't starve, but I had to make a wild dash to the bathroom where my litter box was. That was hazardous, and I almost got caught several times by the littlest one. I managed to train those visitors reasonably well, though, so I wasn't too worried. I threw several loud hissy fits and yowled loudly so they learned to leave me alone. After a week or so, I could come out from under the bed and watch them from my bedroom doorway. I had them pretty much in control. Once in a while, one of them peeked in at me to coo something foolish, but I didn't come out. After a seemingly endless amount of time, they all left, and my cherished silence returned. I can handle comers and goers, but I won't tolerate comers and stayers. Do you blame me?

Third Party Analysis

It seems to me that we have a clear case of confused points-of-view. The humans, rather than train the cat to stop clawing the furniture, took the cat to a veterinarian and had her front claws removed. From a feline point-of-view, it was abuse. From a human point-of-view, it was a necessity. As to the spaying, the same thing: from a feline point-of-view, abuse; from a human point-of-view, necessity.

The problem exists because the humans have not developed an ability to relate to their cat's point-of-view. It is not possible for a feline to relate to a human's point-of-view.

Both sides mention an older cat that apparently left home rather than live with the new Munchkin cat. That appears to have been the beginning of a long-lasting angst. The newest member of the family was cast as an intruder by the older cat, and the humans, perhaps without knowing the source, were drawn into a cat-to-cat issue. This may be the root of the whole familial problem.

Much time must be devoted to retraining within the family unit.

Chapter Two

We Said

We daydream that one day we might take her out for a walk in the woods, sort of like Hansel and Gretel—you know the story, with bread crumbs? Only we won't take the bread crumbs. And she'll get so absorbed in sniffing all the woodsy scents that we'll be able to sneak away, and she'll have no trail of bread crumbs to find her way back. But, alas, we haven't the nerve to try it, because if she did find her way back, she would bite. And if she did bite, we'd have tooth marks and tiny red scratches and holes in our skin.

We daydream that maybe someday we'll have visitors who Boots will like, and maybe she'll go home with them. But so far, the only person Boots liked didn't like her; in fact, that person loathes all cats. When Boots tried to cozy up to her and sit on her lap, she was vigorously shooed away. Yep, you guessed it—under the bed, and mad enough to bite, only we shut the bedroom door quickly so she couldn't come back.

We daydream that maybe someday she'll get married and leave home. It would have to be someone gentle and understanding, so that her peculiarities won't bother him. On that point, consider that if Two Bootie married Doug Flutie, her name would be Two Bootie Flutie. That works, doesn't it?

She Said

As to daydreams, I have them, of course I have them, who doesn't? I dream of having a huge pillow to lie on that will automatically move me to all my sun spots with no effort on my part. My sun spots move from window to window, and I have to get up and follow them. Sometimes I sleep so soundly that when I wake up, my sun spot has moved without me. Sun spots are incredibly warm.

As to my marrying and leaving this place?—I don't think so! I have this family trained just the way I want. And, as to Two Bootie Flutie?—I don't think so!

Third Party Analysis

Daydreams are a normal, healthy method of handling stressful situations. The Hansel and Gretel daydream is a bit worrisome, but it appears to be controlled.

The daydreams reported here are relatively healthy. As long as Boots doesn't act upon them and as long as they don't interfere with healthy interaction between family members, they fit within the normal handling of day-to-day stress.

I do worry about the impractical daydream of an electronic pillow that follows the sun. That takes "unrealistic" to a new high. (Note to myself: consider this further.)

Chapter Three

We Said

Okay, it was a dirty trick to have her front claws removed, but she was tearing up our suede chairs. And how were we to know that removing them would be so traumatic for her?

She Said

Nobody told me I couldn't scratch those chairs. I would have stopped if I had known they were more precious than my front claws ... probably ... maybe.

Third Party Analysis

This is a common problem with feline pets. Cats do have claws, and they do need to use them. The pet owner should have purchased a "scratching log." This would have been, by far, the best solution for the pet; however, it wouldn't have made the home completely safe from claws. If the pet owner makes the decision that clawing the furniture and/or curtains cannot be tolerated on any level, then surgical removal of the claws is a last resort.

Chapter Four

We Said

For several years we had a wonderful, gentle, old, white cat who lived in the house with us. Because we never had any problems with her, we called her our good cat. Boots was merciless about leaping onto her neck and biting her. It was not a nice thing to do.

She Said

That "gentle," old cat didn't like me, so I wanted to bite her, but I didn't; I just wanted to have fun.

Third Party Analysis

A suspected problem here is that there was not enough care taken to introduce the new kitten into the family. A proper introduction takes place over several weeks. The new resident is placed in a separate room, and there is no face-to-face contact between the two. During this period of separation, the two cats can sniff each other through the door separating them and are completely aware of one another with no actual contact. After a week or two of separation, the two cats are, in the best of situations, slowly introduced for mere minutes at the first meeting and longer periods of time over the next few days. This method of introduction removes much of the tension in the home.

It is also suspected that there may have been a bit of competition in the home. The new kitten may have detected a bit of favoritism. A proper handling of the introduction of the two cats would have helped.

Chapter Five

We Said

We have a third cat, Norman, who lives in our garage. It is true that he was hard to get along with at one time. But after he was neutered, he became very docile and gentle. However, Boots still won't let him get near her, even though all he wants now is to touch her nose and say hello. When Boots goes outside the house, all is fine until Norman comes around. Then she goes berserk, making a wild dash to get into the house. If we're not around to let her in, she crawls into a narrow opening under the water heater shelf, and it takes all day to lure her out again.

She Said

That garage cat, Norman, doesn't like me, and if I didn't run he'd tear me to shreds. He's vicious, and I don't give a fig if he has been neutered, he is not gentle and docile. If they want me to go outside and exercise in a normal, healthy fashion, they'll make sure that he stays away from me. I won't play Nosey-Posey with him. I won't!

Third Party Analysis

Again, the initial introduction of Boots and Norman was unfortunate. So much animosity has been created that at this point, there may be no hope for a friendly association between the two. Boots may be forced to remain a house cat while Norman remains ruler of his garage and the outside world.

Chapter Six

We Said

At night, after the lights are out and we're snuggled in our bed, we often whisper to each other that Boots is a funny creature to live with. We really do enjoy seeing her little face when we wake each morning. She follows us around, patiently waiting for her breakfast. While we're eating, she remains nearby lying on her back with all four, short, "munchkin" legs sticking straight up in the air, "guinea pigging," waiting for someone to notice her. Have you ever seen a guinea pig? It's a small animal with fur that grows in swirls. The fur can't be smoothed down because it grows in much disarray. Well, Boots can "guinea pig" her fur. She can make it fluff out, stand up, and swirl in total disarray. Someone once told us that she does this to aerate her body, to cool herself on a warm day. Perhaps. In any case, Boots is talented.

She has another truly amazing talent. Remember, her body is very long, and her legs are very, very short. She can run in two directions at the same time! Really! We've seen her run down the hallway, and while the front half of her body turns west into the kitchen, the back half of her body keeps running north. Boots is, indeed, a gifted cat.

And when we come home tired at the end of the day, there she is, patiently waiting for us at the door. She rolls over onto her side and waits for a scratch. Of course, if we're carrying a large grocery bag—yep, off she goes, under the bed, because bags frighten her.

She's easily coaxed out with a bit of cat food. But, of course, we have to hide the large grocery bag first.

While we're having dinner, Boots sits patiently nearby, waiting for a gentle touch. And when we finish with dinner, she runs down the hallway chortling and cheeping in delight, because she knows her favorite time of day is about to begin.

You see, our life together isn't all bad; she can be quite loveable. In the evening, she'll sit on our laps for as long as we'll sit still, purring so loudly that she can be heard all the way across the room.

She isn't always a bother, except for her little black hairs all over the furniture (and the biting and scratching, of course), and we really wouldn't take her for a drive in the country without bread crumbs—probably.

She Said

I heard that, and I'm glad they like me, because I'm not leaving. I like it under the bed, and I like my sun spots, and I like my Ben Brush, and I like my people ... sometimes.

But next time we write a book, I want to be first: "I said-They said." I don't like being on the defensive.

Third Party Analysis

In a psychologically twisted sort of way, this family seems to have come to a disorganized serenity. It is well documented that there are no set rules for healthy family interaction.

CASE CLOSED.

Chapter Seven

She Said

My favorite part of this whole book is in Chapter Three, where they admit to that dirty trick about my front claws. And, of course, I love that part of Chapter Six where they whisper that they like me.

AND THEY ALL LIVED HAPPILY EVER AFTER.

GRANDMA
FORGETS

How old would you be if you didn't know how old you was?

—SATCHEL PAIGE

Happy Birthday Grandma

Several weeks ago, Grandma wakened from her sleep with a start. Her dream was alarming; she couldn't remember the names of her beloved children, grandchildren and great grandchildren. Could this be a warning of things to come? Oh my, oh my.

As her children had grown into adulthood and given her grandchildren, she worried occasionally that she might forget one of their names. Soon, now, there would be another great granddaughter joining her family. The dream caused her worry. Could she actually forget their names? What to do, what to do?

Each morning since her dream, she awakened with an awful dread. This enormous problem weighed heavily on her. Sometimes through the night, her eyes would fly open with images of all of her loved ones floating before her, and for just a quick moment, she couldn't put names with faces. During these fretful times, she almost had tears in her eyes as she tried to recall their names.

She was blessed with much family, and it distressed her greatly that the years had brought such fuzzy moments. How to solve this predicament?

She made a decision to sit for a period of time every day and think of nothing but her family. She would write down a name and think of the face that matched. This would solve her problem, she just knew it.

That very afternoon, she sat and attempted to write down the names of her children. She drew a blank. Not one of their names came to mind. She stood quickly (well, not so quickly) and walked into her kitchen. She pulled out a pail of peas and started shelling. It was soothing to keep her hands busy. What was wrong with her? Worry, worry!

She needed to think of something that would help sharpen her fuzzy mind. She needed to be assured that she would never, even for a moment, forget one of her children's, grandchildren's or great grandchildren's names.

As the weeks passed, her worry grew. Her ninetieth birthday was approaching, and there was to be a family gathering. It would be a sad occurrence if she forgot someone's name.

She went about her days as usual. Many friends came and went. She had little time to sit and dwell on her problem. But it was never far from her mind. She went to church, visited with friends and family, and she worried. She shopped, visited with the many folks who crossed her path, and she worried. She kept her appointments and visited with her family as they kindly drove her from place to place, and she worried.

Curiously, as she flitted from place to place with her friends and family, Grandma had no difficulty matching names and faces. These were the very same family members who were at the heart of her strange, upsetting quandary. However, when she quieted and remembered the dream, she worried. The human mind is indeed curious!

As her birthday drew nearer, her silent worry became even more intense; her mind was in turmoil. Her worrying persisted through the nights, causing dread. Was there no solution? What a problem, what a problem!

The morning of her birthday she was in such a dither that she could hardly dress. Any minute now, her family would begin arriving to help her celebrate. Why, oh why, had this happened? What could she have done to avoid this problem? In her earlier years, it would never have occurred to her that she would be plagued with a memory problem of this immensity. She sat on her couch and waited anxiously.

Within minutes, she heard a car roll into the driveway. Up she popped (well, not quite popped) to see who had arrived. As she happily greeted John and "Sharon," they hugged her with their eyes twinkling at each other. John was her oldest. Before she completed a proper hello, the door was opened again. When Milton and Cathy were greeted as "Richard" and "Judy," they exchanged secret smiles. When she greeted "Leonard" and "Dallas" and their two children, Connor and Cooper, as they arrived, all four of them had difficulty keeping their smiles hidden.

By now you may be totally confused, because: Robbye is married to John, Sharon is married to Richard, Judy is married to Wayne, Leonard is married to Myra and their children are Adam and Rachel.

Later, Adam came through the door with a grin, as Grandma greeted him with a happy exclamation, "'Lloyd,' you look wonderful, it's so good to see you." The four children standing nearby said, "Uh, oh!"

The rest of her family arrived with a whirl, and she was so busy hugging and being hugged that the hours flew. There were so many to greet. She was indeed a blessed woman. She bent down to straighten the dress of two year old Erin, who giggled at being called "Sierra," then looked up, pleased to see a group of her great grandchildren having a rollicking time in the corner of the room. She couldn't hear them asking each other, with giggles, "What did Grandma call you today?"

But Grandma drew the biggest laugh of the day when she picked up Coti and exclaimed, "'Kaylie,' you're just getting so big, I can hardly pick you up." The whole room dissolved in laughter at the funny look on Grandma's face as she realized what she had done. Her great grandchildren ran to her giggling, "Grandma, you're funny, that's Coti, Kaylie's too big for you to pick up!" Robbye spoke through their laughter, "It doesn't matter what you call us, Mom. It's just wonderful to be with you." And Harold spoke up, "Yep, Mom, we don't care what you call us." Judy melted her worry completely when she hugged her mother-in-law, saying, "That's okay, Esther, we know you love the whole bunch of us, so it doesn't matter who you think we are, we're all yours." (Esther is Grandma's sister.)

Her ninetieth birthday ended with her prayers of thanks to the Lord for all he had given her. She crawled into her cozy bed and just as her eyes closed, she remembered her silly fears. How could she have been so foolish? She had let her fears build into a giant creature that just took over her common sense. Yes, she might forget where she put her glasses but never, never, could she forget her huge, loving family. She might confuse their names, but never the love given to and received from every single one of them. The Lord had blessed her with a marvelous life.

Grandma never lost another moment's sleep over this problem, which turned out to be—NOT A PROBLEM!

NORMAN

AND

MIKIE

(A fairy tale, in part)

Lettin' the cat outta the bag is a whole lot easier 'n puttin' it back in.

—WILL ROGERS

Prologue

On a busy spring day in the year 2003, several of God's hardworking helpers were organizing the list of souls that were to be born the following December. A very clever, older helper, who had a very good memory, realized that there was a connection between one of the new souls, Michael Christopher Schaefer, scheduled to be born on December 14, 2003, and a very old soul, Floyd Oscar Burris, Jr., born on December 14, many years ago.

"Why, I remember him," thought the spry, old fellow, as his memory dredged up old information: Floyd Oscar Burris, Jr., born on December 14, 1942. Deep dimples in both cheeks, large brown eyes with brown hair that fell into one little curl over his forehead—a loveable little boy. Floyd, Jr. was a happy child who asked little for himself. He loved Cheerios for breakfast and Cheerios for lunch. His beloved Cheerios created a great happiness in his life—they did.

The old helper's memory swirled to a morning when a very small Floyd, Jr. tried to pour Cheerios into his cereal bowl. Nothing poured. The box was empty. His little face was etched with sadness. He said nothing. He demanded nothing. He simply sat at the breakfast table in great sorrow. He made no sound as a huge tear formed in the corner of each eye. Within minutes, Floyd Jr.'s sister was out the door, on her way to the store to buy Cheerios. It was a twenty minute walk each way, but the trip was happily made. Such was the charm of the little boy.

When the little boy was given a black Labrador mix puppy, he named the puppy Pancho and for all the boy's growing years, Pancho was his shadow. They played together, they slept together, and when Floyd, Jr. went off to school, Pancho waited patiently at the end of the sidewalk for his companion to return. Pancho was as gentle as the little boy, and the whole Burris family loved to see the two run and play.

As a young man, Floyd, Jr. partially completed his studies. After much hardship, he earned his Bachelor's Degree in chemistry. While in school, he worked full time to support his large family, a wife and four children. He was an unusually quiet young man who rarely spoke an unnecessary word, preferring instead to concentrate on intellectual thoughts. It might be said that he walked with his head in the clouds.

God must have been greatly pleased with Floyd, Jr., for although his life was brief, he completed his mission on earth with honor.

And now the old helper held a new directive in his hands. Michael Christopher Schaefer was to be born on December 14, 2003. For a short while, the old helper had been lost in his memory. But he slowly shook himself back to the present as he realized that if Floyd, Jr. still lived on Earth, he would be Michael's great uncle. Michael was scheduled to be born on his great uncle's birthday.

This was a curious and interesting occurrence. Tucking this tiny information nugget into the back of his mind, the old fellow left, thinking that he really must look up Mr. Burris to see how he was faring. But for now, he had other work to do. He was a very busy man.

Chapter One

On a sultry day in late October 2003, Norman Bates was lying contentedly in the brush in his backyard. Over his lifetime, he had paced many paths through the brush on his property, each one leading to a favorite napping spot. Norman was dreaming his favorite dream while birds chirped above. He had just successfully attacked a plundering canine that had made the mistake of coming onto Norman's private property. Norman vanquished the animal quickly and was drifting into another dreamy sequence about guarding his property from ferocious animals out of the Cleveland National Forest. He drowsily lifted his head and slowly came out of the glories of his dreams. As he looked around curiously, something was wrong. Though Norman's activities on this day were normal, he sensed a peculiar atmosphere.

The people that filled his world were nervous. The back door of the house was opened and closed continuously, and his people came out onto the back deck too often. While on the deck, they looked to the sky as though searching for something. This was unusual. And the streets were filled with many cars coming and going, some of them with noisy sirens. This, too, was unusual. The air was heavy with anxiety.

Finally, in the afternoon, one of Norman's people came out of the house, searched the sky with her eyes, walked down the deck stairs, crossed the yard and gently picked him up. Now, Norman enjoyed being picked up, but this was unsettling. He was always allowed to drowse undisturbed as long as there was daylight.

(Author's Note: By the way, did I tell you? Norman Bates is a cat, an outdoor tabby cat. He lives in a small mountain community with a housebound munchkin cat, Two Boots, and a human family, the Costantinos. Two Boots is afraid of her shadow and is so fearful of the outdoors that she spends all her time inside the house. Norman spends his days outside and his nights in the garage, where he has an electric blanket for cold winters and a comfortable spot in front of a large window for balmy summer evenings. I should caution you this story is a blend of reality and imagination. It might be a mistake to try to sort through the two, so I recommend that you just sit back and let it happen.)

Norman's contentment ended abruptly when the gentle arms placed him in his travel box. He didn't like being put in his travel box, because it meant he would soon have strange people pulling at him and sticking needles into his hip. Not fun. So he started yowling. Norman was soon joined in this noisy activity by the disagreeable Two Boots. She, too, was in her travel box, yowling. Yowling loudly gave them something to do while waiting for the needles.

Today was different though. Usually, the travel box was placed in the car for a short trip, then the strangers with needles, then home again to be released back into the yard, but not today. True, the trip this day was short, but there were no needles, and he wasn't released from his travel box. While Norman and Two Boots were still in their travel boxes, the boxes were taken out of the car and placed on the ground. There, with cats enclosed, they sat. Time dragged. It was all very strange, and the atmosphere was very tense. Norman's people were quiet. Usually they talked so much that at times, he became weary of listening to them, but not today.

The hours wore on, and Norman became acutely uncomfortable. He was offered food and water, but he turned his head away. He wanted out; he wanted to stretch. He wanted to be back in his scrub brush, in his own dirt and on his own property. But this didn't happen. He was trapped, and he didn't understand. Norman Bates was unhappy.

After hours of sitting caged on the ground, the cats were moved back into the car. Norman's spirits lifted, because he thought he would finally be taken home and released. But the car didn't move.

In ordinary times, Norman's life flowed just the way he wanted. His people were so kind that he lived blissfully from day to day with almost never an anxious or upsetting moment. He trusted his people and knew they loved him. But in this particular situation, the behavior of Norman's people was very unusual; he couldn't understand why they would leave him caged for hours on end. But this is exactly what happened. His confusion and physical distress increased by the hour. The whole night passed and still, he was in his travel box.

As the sun came up, there was a heavy smell of smoke and ashes floating in the air. Norman, in his box, was sitting on the ground, with Two Boots trapped in her box beside him. She, too, was confused and uncomfortable. What was happening? Why was it happening? When would it end? And most of all, why were his people doing this to him? Norman Bates was very unhappy.

Late morning on the second day, after Norman had been in his travel box for a full night, for more hours than he could remember, the car finally started moving. "Alright," he thought. "Finally things are going back to normal."

As the car moved, though, Norman knew something was still terribly wrong. His people were still silent. There was no chattering, and the droning of the engine went on and on before the car finally stopped. He could sense from the smell and the feel of the air that he was still in foreign territory. Norman's box was lifted and taken into a strange house. Disappointing! He had been certain that he would soon be home, but this wasn't home; everything was wrong; nothing smelled right; nothing looked right. And, even though the small family was greeted by someone he recognized, Norman still wasn't home. Norman Bates was very, very unhappy.

Norman was rarely distressed, but when he was, he didn't content himself with mere tail switching. He took action with claws and teeth showing, and ferocious growling. But these were his faithful people whom he trusted so much; he could never threaten them with his claws and teeth. It took a fuming Norman some time to work up a serious displeasure with them, but when this final indignation developed, in his acute distress and misery, he thought to himself, "If this box ever opens, I am so outta here, heads will spin. I've protected these people. I've spent practically my whole life keeping our property free from marauding cats and dogs. I was ready to give the rest of my life to these people. But this won't do; it just won't do at all, not at all." His heart was beating so fast, he was almost dizzy with the mighty feelings of anguish and sorrow rushing around in his head.

Chapter Two

In all Norman's tail switching and silent grumbling, he didn't understand that a terrible fire was raging near his home in the Cleveland National Forest. His garage, his deck and all his brushy paths were in danger of burning to the ground. The situation was dire, and all the family's energies were given over to keeping everyone together and safe. Removing Norman and Two Boots from their familiar surroundings and placing them in their travel boxes wasn't a choice, it was a necessity. Norman's understanding was limited, though, so while he fumed and had fearsome, terrible thoughts, his people were trying to help the two cats retain some comfort. They had driven to the home of their son, where they would stay while the forest fire raged.

Norman and Two Boots were carried in their travel boxes to a strange, open area with a high fence. It looked to be a safe place for the cats to roam freely for a while. When the two travel boxes were opened, liberating the cats, timid Two Boots immediately scuttled into a shadowy corner to view the new surroundings, but Norman thought of only two things when his door opened: self-determination and escape. He leaped out and ran to a dark, empty space under a shed. Norman sat crouched in the dark space, plotting his getaway. In his misery, he forgot the kindness of his people friends; he forgot their gentleness; he forgot everything but his own physical distress. His ears were ringing, and he was disoriented from all the momentous happenings. Norman believed that if he could just regain control of his own life, his world would turn upright again, and he could get back to familiar territory. He crept around under the shed and peered out as far as he could see. Everywhere he looked, he saw a tall fence that would be difficult to reach and even more difficult to scale. Norman remained crouched. The human was sitting just beside the shed, and when Norman moved, his human moved with him. It was a standoff between Norman and his man.

As confused as Norman was to be at this precipice in his life, he knew he had no choice. He had to run. And run he did. With no warning to the man, Norman suddenly streaked to a far corner under the shed, bolted out into the open, and leaped onto the top of the shed. From there it was a simple matter to hurdle the tall fence. Norman Bates made his escape. He split. He was free at last.

While his family called for him to come back, Norman, in his haste to escape the outrage of the last two days, ran and ran and ran. He ran until he could no longer run, until finally, he stopped and crept under yet another shed in another yard far away. It was dark, but it wasn't the darkness that crushed him.

As he settled in for a long, lonely night, Norman could hardly breathe. He realized with horror that he had run from the only human friends he had ever had, the people who had protected him, loved him and treated him with kindness. There was no comfort in this strange place, under this strange shed. Comfort was what he had just run from, his people. Norman's head hung low as he muttered to himself, "What to do, what to do?"

Chapter Three

Back in the grassy yard from which Norman had just leaped, the commotion was extraordinary. More family members emerged from the house to help find Norman, but he was nowhere to be found. They looked high and low, but Norman Bates was gone. Their only hope was that Norman would settle down someplace safe and rethink his escape.

Dana, a member of Norman's people family, had come to lend a hand to the wanderers. She was the mother of Michael Christopher (Mikie), who was still nestled safely within her body, unborn but very aware of his surroundings. He could hear and understand a lot of what went on in his presence. Now he was hearing about a great fire (whatever that was) and about Norman Bates, who had leaped over a fence in great distress and couldn't be found. Apparently Norman Bates was someone very important to Mikie's great grandfather.

Mikie didn't know his great grandfather yet, but he could feel the anxiety all the way into his own warm surroundings. He could hear and feel the concerned murmurings of his mother and all the other people, and he began to fear for this Norman Bates. All afternoon, Mikie worried. Where was Norman?

181

It was early evening before Mikie's mother got into her car and started the trip home. She was withdrawn; she didn't speak to him as she usually did. She was quiet. She patted him softly through her tummy, but she was distracted. Could she be worried about Norman Bates? He wondered who Norman was. Maybe she was worried about Mikie's great grandfather. Mikie wondered what a great grandfather was, but whatever he was, Mikie liked it when his great grandfather hugged his mom, Dana. His great grandfather was gentle when he hugged, and he had a soft, quiet chuckle. This Norman must really be something grand to be affecting his mother and great grandfather in this way.

In all his existence in his warm, comfortable cocoon, Mikie had never had reason to think of anyone but his mother and himself. This concern for someone else was new, and it bothered him greatly. He wanted to comfort his mother and his great grandfather, and he wanted to help find this Norman Bates. But how was he to be of any help? He was, after all, not scheduled to make his appearance until December 14th. This was October 28th. Six weeks would pass before he could start helping in the hunt for Norman. Anything could happen in six whole weeks!

Mikie started thinking and plotting. He knew that if he waited the full six weeks for his birth, he would be of no help in the hunt for Norman. On the other hand, Norman might never be found, and Mikie wanted to meet this Norman Bates whom his great grandfather held in such high esteem.

Mikie had his very first hero! Norman Bates. And he wanted to be of use—he knew he could be of use—to his great grandfather and to Norman Bates. Mikie had a mission.

Chapter Four

Mikie had little understanding of the world he was soon to enter. He knew it would be different from his present existence. His mother had promised it would be exciting. She had promised that she would help him all the way. She had promised he would be able to do anything he set out to do, and he believed everything she told him. Mikie didn't yet know what his strengths and limitations might be, but he knew his mother was his link to the new world. She was his most important person. Therefore, he had to find a way to let her know of his mission, but how to do this? When his mother spoke to him, he could roll over or kick his legs or stretch his arms out. He could respond to her, but could she respond to him? He didn't know. Mikie had to get his mother's attention. He had to let her know that he needed to speed up his entry into her world.

Mikie had to be born now. Just exactly what "being born" meant was a mystery to him, but he sort of thought it was a kind of journey. Part of the mystery was how he could journey anywhere. The only world he knew was very small. Actually, it was only large enough for him to roll around. And when he kicked his feet or flailed his arms, he always hit the walls. So the idea of a journey confused him.

Mikie pondered. He thought of his mother singing to him and talking to him. "I've got it," he thought. "I'll talk to her." He called out, "Mom? Ma! Can you hear me? I've got a job to do, and I can't do it in here. I need to get out. Now! If you can hear me, rub your tummy." Nothing, he got no response. "Hum," he thought. "Maybe I'll get her attention if I can make her feel me. Maybe I should get physical." So he rolled around a bit, nothing. Then he stuck out his foot as far as he could. That brought an "ouch" from his mother, but still she didn't really seem to be communing with him. He stretched out his whole body as far as he could. And then he drew himself into a tight ball and rolled around twice.

At last, she started talking to him. But it wasn't a two-way conversation. She was talking, but she wasn't listening. Although Mikie was a bit dizzy from all the rolling, he still tried to get his mother to hear him. But she didn't. She continued talking to him, but when he responded, she didn't hear. "Ma, I'm worried about Norman Bates. I'm worried about my great grandfather. I can't wait until December 14th. I need to be born now! Ma, I want to help. Mom, I've got a mission!" Nothing.

But at least when Mikie rolled, she talked to him. So he continued to roll, and kick, and flail his arms, and nudge with his fanny. He actually made himself a bit sick to his stomach with all his activity.

In his frantic activity, Mikie lost track of time, but finally, after several exhausting weeks of physical exertion, he heard his mother speaking with her doctor. The conversation seemed to be about bringing on an early labor (whatever that was). The only word Mikie knew was "early" and that made his little heart beat faster, and he sang out, "Okay Norman, I'm outta here! Keep your spirits up, I'm coming. Stay alive, Norman. I'll find you. No matter how long it takes, stay alive, I'll find you. Whatever you do, just stay alive. I'm on my way."[1]

---

[1] Hawkeye to Cora in James Fenimore Cooper's *Last of the Mohicans*.

Chapter Five

When Norman Bates made his leap for freedom, he was full of confused fury. But it quickly turned to a weary sadness as he thought of his life without his chosen people. With them he had fresh food and water twice a day. He had his very own wooden deck where he could keep watch over his land. From his deck he had a clear view of all his land, so he could see and ward off usurpers before they could cause his people or property any harm.

Norman's homeland was peppered with trees, bushes and grass, so when he wanted to nap he had his choice of many sunny and shady spots. When it rained, he had a small house to keep him dry, or he could stay in his garage until the rain stopped. When the wind blew, he almost always was placed in the garage and sheltered from the sounds and forces that frightened him.

When the sun went down, he went into his garage where, on cold nights, he had his own electric blanket to keep him warm. Or he could leap up to his window seat and keep watch out the window while he catnapped.

And always, always, there was the warmth of his humans. In his earlier years, Norman had been out in the world, and he knew the value of these people. What had he done?

On that terrible day when Norman's life was shattered and he made his great escape, he just wanted to run and run and run. When he finally stopped running and crept under that dark shed with his heart almost broken by disappointment, Norman knew he was in trouble. He knew he had made a mistake.

Norman slept fitfully until daylight. He had a dreadful dilemma: should he keep moving, or should he try to find his way back to his people? His mind had been racing all night, and he knew he had to find a safe shelter and food and water soon. He watched carefully from under the shed to see what dangers were in his way. He saw numerous cats, dogs and people, none of whom were bothered by his scent or presence. Without really making up his mind about which way to go, Norman ventured forth to scout the land.

He had learned not to trust strange humans, so he kept out of their way. He did not trust dogs, so he kept careful watch for them. He knew cats could be helpful, but they could also be treacherous. This was a new and dangerous world.

Norman Bates' first day in this dangerous world was spent moving from dark spot to dark spot. Watching, always watching, for dangers in the shape of humans, dogs, cats, bikes and automobiles. For the last few years, Norman's days had been spent on his own property where quiet reigned, except for an occasional neighboring cat or dog out for a walk. In this new world, the atmosphere was teeming with noises that were loud and vexatious. It sapped his energy. When dusk fell that first day of "freedom," Norman was hungry but relieved when he found a small building off by itself from which he could see in all directions. He crept under the building and settled down for another fitful night of watching and dreaming. Norman dreamed of the touch of his people. His dreams were so real that he awoke with a start, thinking he was back home. But he wasn't; he was alone.

Norman's second day of freedom in his now more familiar, but still dangerous, neighborhood was spent canvassing for food sources. In his movements of the day, he had seen food bowls, but he made no attempt to eat from them. There was too much activity that he didn't trust. Hunger was bothering him today, though, and he was more determined. Water was plentiful, as were mice and birds. However, mouse hunting would use up energy that Norman was trying to preserve. Bird hunting would inevitably make noise and a flurry of activity that would cause the attention he wanted to avoid. The first bowl of food that Norman came across was inedible. It was dog food. The second bowl was empty. The third and fourth bowls were dog food. Apparently, in this neighborhood, dogs were better fed than cats. In late morning, Norman found a bowl of cat food and was just settling down to enjoy when he heard the familiar hiss and spit of a cat.

He scampered away, and the hissing cat didn't follow, so Norman quickly went on his way. He hadn't gone far when he spotted another food bowl, but it too was empty. He sat for a while to rest and think. Luckily, he sat long enough to see a door open and a woman quietly come out to fill the bowl with fresh cat food. She saw him and spoke so softly that he felt no threat from her. He ventured to the bowl, ate his fill and rapidly leaped away to a secure spot where he could think over his situation. Though Norman was stressed in this strange neighborhood, he wasn't ready to go back to the yard from which he had run because he still couldn't understand the actions of his people.

Norman, however, did have some critical thinking to do. He didn't have a constant source of food. Water seemed to be plentiful, but venturing out into the open to drink was dangerous. The weather was turning cold, and he knew it would soon be rainy. He hadn't had a real deep sleep since he was wrenched from his mountain home, and his strength was faltering. He was in trouble. He had been in trouble before, though, and he could do this. He knew he could. With a lump in his throat and a heavy heart, Norman decided he couldn't go back. Once this decision had been made, he considered seriously whether he wanted to live outside permanently, or whether he wanted to attempt hunting for a new family.

Chapter Six

On his third day of freedom, Norman opted to live outside in the neighborhood yards. He couldn't bring himself to consider looking for new people. With his hunger satisfied, he was rejuvenated; he would make a home for himself by himself. He would start life anew. In his scouting, he had ventured onto the rim of a canyon, and that was his first choice. He could live on the edge of the canyon, just deep enough to be safe from dogs, humans and other cats, but not so deep as to run into the unspeakable horrors that he knew were there. Remember, Norman had lived on the edge of the Cleveland National Forest; he knew what lived behind that green screen of trees.

Norman's idea of living on the edge of the canyon didn't work. The first night trying to sleep was terrible. Tiny, vicious, venomous, insects burrowed into his skin, biting and making him itch. And he saw loathsome creatures slink out of the dark shadows, spreading an awful stench. The horrors of Norman's mountain forest were nothing compared to this terrible place. Reluctantly, he decided he would try neighborhood life, after all.

Earlier in his life, Norman had been an unattached neighborhood cat, and he knew about that life. It was a hard life, especially if there was no special house where a bit of temporary safety could be found. So, he set out to charm women, men and children with the hope of being accepted, but nothing worked for him. For some strange reason, Norman's charm didn't work in this neighborhood. He tried talking to women, and they shook their brooms at him. He tried playing with old people, and they yelled at him. He tried winding around men's legs, and they kicked at him. He tried peeking at children, and they threw things at him. These reactions confused Norman. Finally he remembered there had been one woman who had fed him, who had spoken so softly that he didn't fear her.

Chapter Seven

It took Norman a few days to find the house again, and by the time he reached it, he was weak with exhaustion and hunger. He crept into the shadow of a fence to wait. While he waited, he saw many cats, but one in particular interested him. The cat seemed to live in a nearby house. His fur was long and gray, and he had a knowing glint in his eye. This strange cat was comfortable in the neighborhood and liked to sit in the middle of the street. People driving along the street were careful as they passed him by.

Grady was his name, and of course, Grady knew of Norman's distress; he had seen Norman jump the fence many days ago. Grady knew everything that went on in his neighborhood. He was well acquainted with the cats who lived nearby. He knew which of them lived outside and which lived inside. He knew all the dogs in the neighborhood and made it his business to keep them respectful of him.

Grady decided he liked Norman Bates. He had enjoyed Norman's "leap to freedom," and he liked Norman's courage. Grady wanted Norman as a buddy. He started his friendship with a "silent watching." Silent watching is universally understood in the cat world. The watching can go on for a short period of time or a long period of time, since cats are very patient. Grady knew that Norman had been out in the weather for many days, so after an hour of silent watching, he decided he would take control of the situation. He ended his watch, walked up to the house, and made a noisy nuisance of himself. The woman immediately opened her door to invite him in, but Grady refused to enter.

The friendly woman, somewhat irritated by Grady's refusal, came out to fill the bowl with cat food, went back into the house, and shut the door. Without eating, Grady moved back from the bowl of food and resumed his silent watch. After a short while, he moved several feet further away, always keeping his eyes on Norman. Cat-to-cat, this was a signal that Norman was free to eat the food. So he did. After his meal, Norman ventured slowly toward Grady and they sat, watching one another silently.

Grady and Norman began a tentative friendship—tentative because Norman wasn't comfortable with anyone yet, especially another cat. But he did appreciate Grady's gesture and knew he had a friend—maybe.

(Author's Note: How to explain Norman's reluctance to return to his beloved people? Well, we can't. Norman, like all cats, is mercurial and aloof and never, never lets on what lurks in his heart and mind. We hope hubris won't be his downfall.)

Chapter Eight

Even though Norman Bates now had two allies in the neighborhood, he still wasn't comfortable. The weather had turned quite cold, and the rain would soon follow. His days were filled with moving from place to place, keeping out of the way of humans and dogs. His nights were filled with keeping warm and dry and trying to catch cat naps. The life of a wanderer turned out to be harder than he remembered.

Norman was rethinking his earlier decision to make a new life as an unattached neighborhood cat. If he hadn't been so determined to make his own way, he might be rethinking all of his decisions of late. He felt his sorrow and loneliness deeply as he realized anew that most humans weren't drawn to him. His only safety was with the kindly woman who fed him. However, several cats already lived with her, and they were no friendlier than the rest of the neighborhood. Grady was different. He had become a friend, but he had limitations.

Norman rested in Grady's neighborhood for more than a week. When he regained his strength, he decided it was time to move on. He left the friendly woman and Grady's now familiar streets, traveling for what seemed to be a great distance. He kept in the shadows, knowing this was his best course. He traveled past the canyon rims where the unspeakables lived. As he traveled past the house from where he had made his escape, he watched longingly for his people, but the house was dark. He didn't see anyone.

Norman couldn't have known, but the fire had been contained for some time now. His people had returned to their mountain home, seventy miles away. He also couldn't know that his people returned daily to roam the streets calling for him, while he roamed the streets looking for a suitable place to relocate. He wasn't hearing their calls for him, "Norman, are you there? Come on, Norman. Here kitty, here kitty. Norman, where are you?"

Norman moved through the neighborhood, unaware of the search for him, sorrow causing his head to drop and his tail to drag. He missed his people—until he remembered. That was gone now. He must make a new life.

As he traveled, Norman realized he didn't like any of the yards. And with minor variations, all the neighborhoods were alike; there were cats, dogs, children and cars. As he traveled, Norman carried a large burden: memories were heavy on his heart, and he was still desolate. Sometimes the sound of a man's voice or a woman laughing made him stop and listen—until he remembered. That was gone now. He must make a new life.

He traveled in the dark of night, crawling under buildings for short catnaps. When the rains started, Norman's gloom grew. A cold, wet cat is one of God's most miserable creatures. Cats don't like to be wet. Norman Bates didn't like to be wet, but wet he was. For three whole days and nights, the skies opened, and if it wasn't raining heavily, it was drizzly. The ground was mushy, and no one had time for a wet, dejected cat. There were no kindly women to feed a hungry cat; there were no friendly Gradys to keep a lonely cat company.

The rains finally stopped, and Norman was able to curl up in a relatively dry and quiet spot for the evening. He was so exhausted emotionally and physically that he slept soundly—too soundly. His dreams were filled with the feel of his humans and his old home: he was lying contentedly on his deck, right in the middle of a sun spot. The sun was so warm that he slowly turned over to lie on his back with the sun warming his tummy. As dawn came, he stretched and opened his eyes to the soft, first sunlight of the day only to leap in terror yowling, "Holy cow, holy cow!" The sounds that tore from his throat shocked him. He had awakened to a set of eyes gazing into his face, close enough to do him great bodily harm. Luckily it was only a passing, curious black crow, but Norman was shaken to his core. He had been so deep into his dream of his old home and old humans that he had let down his guard and placed himself in grave danger. This wouldn't do; it simply would not do.

As Norman shook off his disgust with himself, he realized finally that he didn't fit anywhere anymore. He decided that he might just as well travel back to Grady and the kindly woman. At least in Grady's territory, he had regular meals. His long journey back was miserable, but he made it after several long, dreary hours of traveling in the shadows.

Grady greeted him with his normal passivity, but he was helpful in getting Norman a full bowl of food. The friendly woman filled the bowl, and after the experience of the last few days, Norman almost felt he was back home—but not really.

Chapter Nine

While Norman Bates was dealing with his problem, Heaven was moving along, well, heavenly. Suddenly, there came from one of the Heavenly offices a loud exclamation, then the sound of rustling paper and running feet. The sound of telephones ringing and printers ratcheting out paper made a furious flurry of activity.

Soon the activity quieted down enough that God's helpers could absorb the news. It didn't happen often with such short notice, but apparently a recent directive that was well on the way to be being completed had been abruptly updated. Michael Christopher Schaefer, who had been scheduled to be born on December 14, 2003, was on his way—now—and would be born early, on December 5, 2003. The old helper stood amidst all the hurrying and worrying and hand wringing. Right in the middle of the room he stood with a puzzled expression on his face. All of a sudden, he snapped his fingers and exclaimed, "I've got it. I remember. Floyd Oscar Burris, Jr., December 14, 1942. He's Michael's great uncle. That's right!" He rushed over to a file cabinet and pulled out a file. "See, it's right here. I knew it."

No one turned. No one was interested. The early birth of a soul was so exciting that no one had time to look back. The old helper looked around and realized that his information was interesting only to himself. Now that a new date had been set, no one cared that an uncle and a great nephew had almost shared a birthday. The old helper smiled to himself. He knew someone who would be interested. He pulled out his cell phone and made a call.

Chapter Ten

Early on December 5, 2003, a full nine days before his expected arrival, Michael Christopher Schaefer was born.

It had taken the old helper a couple of days to reach his party, so it wasn't until December 7th that the old fellow stood quietly with a handsome, young companion, watching from above the doings in a hospital room. All had been quiet for some hours. A young woman was sleeping and so was her new son. Floyd Burris, Jr. was watching the scene in a quandary. He didn't want to be impolite, but he really didn't have the time to stand watching a scene that held no interest for him. The old man who had guided him to this site was so delighted with himself, though, that there was nothing to do but allow the moment to last. So they watched silently, Floyd, Jr. with little interest and, admittedly, with just a touch of pique.

The door swung open and three people entered: an elderly man, an elderly woman and a younger man. The young mother glowed with excitement in showing off her new baby. The old woman went to the baby, and Floyd, Jr. was immediately electrified. He turned to the old helper, saying, "I know her. That's my sister, that's my sister. She's so old, but I know her. That's Rachel."

"Of course, that's why we're here, so you can see your earthly family. The baby, Michael, was originally scheduled to be born on your birthday, and I remembered you from all those years ago when you first came to us. Michael's birth date changed, but I thought you might be interested."

"And look, that's Ralph. I know him too. I would know them anywhere, but how they've aged. I've followed my own children and grandchildren, watched them grow, but I didn't know I could see the rest of my family like this. Who's the baby? Who's the baby's mother? Is that Rachel's daughter? And who's the fellow that came in with them?"

The old helper quietly answered Floyd, Jr.'s questions. "The young mother, Dana, is your sister's oldest granddaughter, and the baby is Dana's newborn son, Michael. The younger man with them is your nephew, David," the old helper said, while thinking to himself, "My goodness, what has he been doing these last thirty-plus years? I always forget that not everyone is still involved with the doings on Earth." "You do remember Rachel and Ralph have three children, don't you?"

Floyd, Jr. stood with rapt attention as he watched the scene before him. He watched his sister with wonder as he realized that, though aged, she actually hadn't changed at all. It crossed his mind that she would probably read to little Michael, as she had read to him all those years ago. He still remembered two of his favorite books, "The Little Engine That Could" and "The Pokey Little Puppy." He drew up the memory of the little white puppy with brown (or was it gray?) spots on the cover of the book. Oh, how he had loved to have those stories read to him.

The old helper chuckled at the reaction. Floyd, Jr. obviously had never considered that, unlike himself, his earthly family members were now senior citizens. Sometimes the old helper wondered how intellectuals spent their time in Heaven. He was always surprised at what they didn't pay attention to. He left Floyd, Jr. in silence, for he had other work to do. He was a busy man.

As long as his earthly family stayed in the hospital room, Floyd, Jr. watched with fascination. He watched his little great nephew and remembered sensations and feelings that he hadn't felt in tens of years. It was so different in Heaven. What an interesting experience to be thrown back to those days on Earth. As his sister left the hospital room, Floyd turned and slowly walked away with his thoughts far away in time. He hesitated only long enough to make sure that his old friend, Pancho, was following.

Chapter Eleven

Norman's experiences of the last few weeks had made him remember. He remembered sleeping in an airy garage with an occasional mouse to catch. If the weather was wet or cold, he had a warm shelter in his garage with an electric blanket to keep him warm. He had food and water bowls that were always filled. During the day, he had his own property to roam, and he always knew that he was "King of the Hill." He could sit on his deck and watch the whole of his world, keeping it safe from interlopers.

Norman finally allowed himself to really remember his people. They never hurt him. They never turned him away. They never kicked him or threw things at him. His woman person wasn't good for scratching, but sometimes she tried, and she talked to him when they worked in the garden together. Two Boots was unpleasant, but at least her habits were predictable; he knew what she would and wouldn't do.

Most important though was his best person, his man. Norman missed him. He missed his voice. He missed his touch. He missed his smell. He missed the yard work they did together. He missed most of all the times when only the two of them would just sit and scratch; the man would scratch as long as Norman would lay still. And the man liked to listen to Norman talk. Norman liked to talk a lot, and he liked to talk loud. In these last three weeks, he had discovered that not everyone liked his voice. As a matter of fact, no one liked his voice except his own people. Norman Bates wanted to go home.

Norman didn't know how to return to the house from which he had run so long ago. He knew it was near, but in his moving around, he had always avoided that yard because it reminded him of the "inhumane treatment" of his people toward him. Norman's point of view was a bit different now. Until the last three weeks, he had led a good life. Could it be that he didn't know the whole story? Could there have been something that he had missed? Could he have been wrong? Maybe he had been rash in his haste to get away.

The evening was early, still light, and Norman wasn't particularly hungry, so he immediately leaped up onto the top of the tallest fence he could find. It was a good height to view the neighborhood. It was the best way to find the yard from which he had escaped so many days ago. As Norman leaped, he heard a sound that was familiar. It sounded like someone was calling his name. He knew that voice. He meowed loudly. While he meowed, he kept moving. He heard it again. He did. "Norman, Norman, are you out there?" "I'm here," he howled, "I'm here." From where was the voice coming? Norman cried, "Wait, I'm coming." In his haste, he fell off the fence and scrambled back to the top, howling all the way. The voice was closer, so Norman called again, "Wait for me. Don't go. I'm here." Norman was past caring where he ran, and when he thought he saw something in a shadow, he leaped off the fence, running toward it. He didn't know where he was, nor did he care. He was running toward the rest of his life. Norman saw a woman, and she was familiar. He kept moving toward her, not even aware that he was out in the open. The woman was standing in a light. Norman moved faster and faster. When he reached her, she kneeled down and said, "Norman, is that you? Norman?" She scooped him up, and the feeling of her was good. As he pushed his face into her shoulder, he was beyond crying; he was cradled carefully. The woman turned and yelled loudly, "Ralph, Ralph, can you hear me? I've got Norman. I've got him, I've got him."

Finally, after dozens of trips down from the mountain and across the city to search for him, the woman quickly carried Norman through the door, into that strange house, out another door and back into the night air. She placed the cat in Ralph's arms, and when Norman felt the warm, familiar, loving arms encircle him, he turned and clutched at the figure that he had missed so dreadfully. His claws sank into the man's shoulders, and he held on tight. He felt the love.

Chapter Twelve

Norman was in a haze. He thought he was in a fantasy. The long ride home would forever be filmy in his mind. The voices of his people were just as he had dreamed. Their talking lulled him into a luxurious, relaxed state. He was safe. For the first time in three weeks, Norman Bates was safe. Forever after, he would remember his fear that the ride home was a dream until he touched his own property, his own dirt. He knew the smell. He knew the feel of home. And when he finally knew he was home on his own territory, with his own people, when he finally knew his wandering was over, all he wanted was his electric blanket. He crawled up onto his blanket and he stayed there for a full day, soaking in the warmth. Norman Bates was happy.

On the second beautiful morning after his homecoming, Norman walked the whole expanse of his property. He walked his cherished brush paths whispering to himself, "There's no place like home."[2] And as he reached each of the four corners of his property, he stopped and whispered to himself, "There's no place like home." And as he circled each familiar tree and shrub that had now

---

[2] Dorothy, from *The Wizard of Oz*.

become so beloved to him, he whispered to himself, "There's no place like home." Norman Bates was home.

Epilogue

Mikie was befuddled from his birth journey for the first couple of days; therefore, it was not until early evening on December 7th that he remembered Norman Bates and his mission. He was in a deep sleep when he heard a familiar voice. It warmed his heart. It was gentle, and he heard a soft chuckle. Where had he heard that sound before? Finally, he remembered. His memory snapped into shape. Norman Bates! That was it. No! Not Norman Bates, his great grandfather. He would know that chuckle anywhere. Wow! He'd made it! Now he could start on his mission to help find this Norman Bates. He lay very still and listened to the conversation swirling around him. Finally he heard the conversation turn to something called a fire. Then he heard the words, "You found Norman? When did you find him? Where did you find him?" His mom's voice was excited, so Mikie lay quietly, with fixed attention, listening to his great grandpa's story of Norman's adventure.

His hero had beaten the odds and survived! His joy at the news overshadowed any anguish he felt at not being able to participate in the hunt. What was important was that Norman Bates had been found, safe.

As he lay quietly, listening to the conversation between his mother and great grandfather, Mikie slowly came to the realization that even if he had been born when he first became aware of Norman's problems, he wouldn't have been able to help in the hunt. He kicked his legs and realized he didn't quite know how to control them; he shook his arms and realized he didn't quite know how to work them. He didn't even know how his fingers worked. "Well, shoot, darn, phooey," whispered Mikie to himself. "I'm not much in the hero department, yet, but I will be. I will be. 'As God is my witness,'[3] someday I will be a hero, just like my idol, Norman Bates."

AUTHOR'S NOTE

Three almost interconnected lives: Floyd Oscar Burris, Jr., who left this earth before he could become a great uncle, but who lives forever in the hearts of those who knew him; Michael Christopher Schaefer, a brand new soul who almost shared his birthday with his unknown great uncle; and Norman Bates, a tabby cat. In time, Michael and Norman did finally meet, but that's another story for another day.

And, of course, as Michael's life unfolds, how many brave and heroic actions will we have to write about? Remember, Michael made a personal vow to be a hero

---

[3] Scarlet O'Hara in, *Gone With the Wind*.

someday! Of course, hopefully, Mikie's understanding of "hero" will mature somewhat.

EARP

I believe cats to be spirits come to earth. A cat, I am sure, could walk on a cloud without coming through.

—JULES VERNE

A Good Life

I started out in a small mountain community called Julian, California, but I don't remember Julian; my first memories are of Pine Valley. For a time I had a twin sister, and I remember her mainly because she looked just like me and because she always walked behind me. I enjoyed her because no matter how I treated her, she still followed me (like Little Feather/Norman Bates followed me, but that's a whole 'nother story).

My twin and I had a good life. We lived with Terry and Jim, who had a houseful of little girls. My twin would keep them happy by letting them dress her up in baby clothes and carry her around. She kept me free from those activities, but after she disappeared, they insisted on dressing me in those clothes. You just can't avoid three of them—little girls, that is—so I had to let them stuff me into the baby clothes and wrap me in pink blankets. I didn't like it, but they were nice little girls and the blankets were soft.

Terry was a nice lady, and I did like her and all the family, but she had eyes like an eagle and she kept a tight rein on me. I've always loved being out at night, especially when the moon was full, but for the first few years, Terry wouldn't let me out after dark. Every single night, whenever I could maneuver near the door—every single time—Terry would shriek, "Shut that door, don't let that cat out." It makes me cringe even now just to think about it. Whew, hurt my ears!

My twin and I used to walk the trails outside of the family property. We would walk single-file along the property line, and since we did it twice every day, we had a deep rut worked in the tall grass, so we felt secure. I always went first, and she came several feet behind me. I looked tough with my head down and my walk was really smooth, you know ... slow and methodical and rhythmic.

Ralph (more about him later) once said I had a John Wayne Walk, whatever that was. It was a good act because right behind me, my twin was trying to do the same thing. Of course, she was a bit smaller, and she couldn't bring off the tough look that I could. But she tried, and we knew we looked bad because we caused a commotion when the neighbors were out in their yard: they would point and talk about us. And their grandkids would try to chase us, but we never got caught unless we wanted to.

Every morning we went out after the mist dried off the grass and we slept all day in our private spots. Ah, the contentment of those private spots: there were bugs and butterflies and bees to keep us entertained, and the sun would filter down through the brush and burn into our fur. The silence was good. Then in the late afternoon, after musking all day, we would take the same trail back home through the tall grass. It was a good life.

But then my sister disappeared and I was all alone. Actually, it was okay with me; sure I missed her, but all I did was sleep all day so I didn't need a partner.

After a few months, the family brought home some kittens—a black one and a striped one. It was good in one way because then I didn't have to let the little girls dress me up anymore. The kittens were perfect for that job. I was left alone for some weeks, and then the kittens started to follow me out to the trail. At first, they were easily distracted because they chased each other and tussled around so much that I could lose them. But as the weeks went by, they worked harder at following me, and I really didn't like that. I was used to my solitary walk and my quiet afternoon musk naps, and I didn't want my routine changed. The two were always together, and I used to watch them from behind the tall grass. They would roll around, jumping out of the grass and scaring each other. It looked like they enjoyed themselves. But one day, just like my twin, the little black one disappeared. Again, I didn't miss him, but it did cause a problem because then the striped one concentrated on me. I really, really didn't like that. By that time he had a name, Little Feather, and by the way, my name was Chiawacha. I think it's Indian for Big White Mountain or some such thing.

At some point, I started getting a tug deep within me, that there was something interesting at the house behind us. I didn't know what it was; probably it was a cat thing. At about the same time, Terry's family became disrupted: if we weren't careful, we'd get locked out at night. That would have been just fine, but it was winter. I liked my life with the family because I liked Jim, the big one. He was only there in the morning and at night, but his voice was gravelly, and I liked his smell; I used to show off for him. Also, the little girls were more or less quiet when he was home. But he began staying away often, so I started on a scouting trip.

I don't know if you've ever gone out scouting, but it's a hard job, and if you do it right, it takes a long time. I was curious about the guy at the house in back of Terry and Jim's, but still I walked all around the neighborhood to make sure that I liked him. After a few weeks I did settle on his house for several reasons: 1) peace and quiet, 2) there was a nice high deck to lay on and I could look out on all the property, 3) the little girls that visited didn't stay long, 4) the lady that lived there didn't swing a broom at me, 5) no cats, 6) no dogs, and finally, and best of all, 7) being near, and watching the guy. Ralph touched something deep inside me. Curious, but there it was; and then, too, I liked guys with gravitas. All in all, I had a good feeling.

First, I watched from the tall grass for weeks to catch the guy's routine. I didn't want to go in too soon and be wrong about him. Remember, I was leaving noise, cats and girls; I wanted a quiet house with, above all, no cats.

The guy intrigued me, but it was the sturdy little lady that spotted me first. She seemed okay with me, so I started moving in closer. After a few weeks, I left the tall grass for short periods of time and watched her from the property line. She knew I was there and wasn't bothered by me, so I started watching her from under her deck. That was a good spot because Little Feather was afraid to follow me. The lady was okay with this too, but I didn't get close for several weeks. I wanted to be sure I was making a good move. After some time, I moved in a little closer to see what she would do, and I'll be darned if she didn't start bringing ham out to me—good ham, too. The guy, Ralph, just ignored me. I'm not even sure he saw me, but I was watching the way he moved and sounded, and he was big and quiet. I was pretty sure I had made a good choice.

We watched each other for several weeks, Rachel, that's her name, and I. Ralph still seemed to ignore me, which I thought curious because I felt he knew I was there. So I would go up and sleep by Rachel while she worked outside; she liked me. Then when the weather got cold, she stayed in the house, but she would leave the door open for me. I started going in to watch her cook. Rachel was always cooking something, and I liked the way the house smelled. She let me roam around the house and rub all the walls and furniture. Once, just for effect, I sprayed one of the bathroom heaters, but, WHEW! Did that cause trouble? Uh-huh! I don't know what the problem was; I thought my mark smelled good, but the commotion Rachel made was awesome! I decided not to do that again.

Well, it seemed like a good place to live, but I needed to get to know Ralph. I needed to know about the connection I felt with him. He ignored me and though he knew I was there, he wouldn't show it. Maybe I was wrong—maybe he was a dog person!

So one warm afternoon, I watched him for hours, trying to figure out what it was about him that felt so right deep inside me. He was outside, just sitting on a small stool, staring out into space. He didn't move for a long time, so I just waited. Finally, he dropped his head into his hands and looked just like I felt when I realized that Little Feather was here to stay—you know, forlorn. So I had no choice, I took the BIG STEP. I walked around him several times and he still didn't notice me, so I walked right up to him and pulled my best trick. It was a real show stopper and it never failed. I got right in front of him so he couldn't miss me and dropped right at his feet with a thump! It worked just like I knew it would. He started laughing just like I knew he would. So I rolled over on my back and showed him my belly. He laughed and laughed and started rubbing my belly fur; he even picked me up and rubbed my back fur. Now, I don't like being picked up: it's a cat thing, but with Ralph, it felt good. I knew then I had a home and a mission. I only needed to make the gradual transfer.

I started staying later and later with Ralph. I believe he would have let me stay as late as I wanted, but with Little Feather meowing outside the window, he always put me out the door when it got dark.

I decided that I had to insist. So, one day when it started snowing heavily, I stayed on Ralph's porch. It was cold and wet, but I hoped it would let him know I meant to move in. By the time he got home, I looked stiff with cold and even whiter than normal with snow. As you well know, cats have heavy fur and I actually enjoyed cold weather most of the time, but I made myself look miserable by crowding up next to the screen door on the porch. When they got home, Rachel clucked and cooed and Ralph brought me into the house. He got a nice thick towel and dried my fur and then called Terry to come get me. After a while, one of the little girls came after me, but I knew I would do it again and again.

After a few more days I went out in a drenching rain and sat huddled on the deck rail while Ralph ate his breakfast. He let me in, dried me off and called Terry again. Of course, she wasn't home (I already knew she was gone for the day) so he kept me in. I stayed all day and spent the night with him. He let me sleep on his bed too!

I tried living with Ralph on and off for several weeks and loved it. I still went to Terry and Jim's often just to keep them happy, but their house was too uncomfortable now.

I loved the Costantino winter routine. It was cold outside, so most nights after they got home from work, we would have dinner and then just go to bed and watch TV. I loved running down the hall with them. Of course I was faster than them, and I would jump into bed even before they reached the bedroom. It was going to be a very good life.

Just as I decided on my own to move in permanently, I heard Terry talking with Ralph; I heard her say they were moving and I could stay with Ralph. YESSS!

But with life, you just never know what's around the corner. My life was just perfect—new home, new guy, no Little Feather. And what do they do? They walk in with a kitten. Why? What was going on? They had me! Of all the loathsome things they could do—a black cat. Cute, really cute!

Well, I pulled out. That very day, I left for good. There were more homes in Pine Valley than I could count, and I could go into almost any one of them and be lots happier than in that "cat" house. April was a bad time for Ralph to do this to me because it was wet out, but I was determined.

You know, I was so sure of Ralph that I kept coming back to see if he was sorry; to see if the black thing was gone. But he kept it, can you believe that? He kept it even after I left.

Terry and Jim hadn't moved yet, so I tried going back with them, but there was too much turmoil. I scouted the house across the street, but something didn't feel right. I scouted all around the neighborhood, but nothing was right. I could have moved in with any number of families, but none of them felt as good as Ralph. It sticks in my craw to say it, but it's true, I did like him. Every few days I would check to see if the black creature was gone, but he kept it. I guess there's just no accounting for taste.

Ralph came down to visit me one day while I was sleeping on Terry's deck, and I knew when I saw him coming through the back fence that he was sorry about bringing home the black thing. So, since I was spending all of my time outside in the cold and rain; and since I knew Ralph was sick with worry, I decided to give him another try. By that time, surely he knew that we didn't need that black thing. True happiness was Me, He and She. "It" could go.

Well, things didn't work out that way. It stayed. Such are the vicissitudes of life. So I showed it who was boss and it left me alone most of the time. Its name was Two Boots. By the way, Ralph gave me a new name: Earpie. Earp. I sort of liked it. I never understood why, but Rachel called me Herpie, their grandkids called me Aunt Earpie and my doctor called me Ear Pie. Go figure. Before I close the subject of the black fur bag, let me make it clear that it did not sleep on Ralph's bed; it slept on the floor or under the bed. I settled in to stay, and once again, life was good. I got used to the black thing and it amused me. It chased me around, but when I was through with the game, all I had to do was stop and look at it; it whimpered and ran under the bed.

Somewhere in there my gender changed. I started out as a male, I think. And my doctor thought I was a male. But Ralph thought I was a female. And as I said before, the grandkids called me Aunt Earpie. Ahhh, what the hell's the difference? I didn't care, but it was confusing.

We worked out a satisfactory routine. I got fed on time, got petted and scratched regularly, got lots of sleep in a warm, safe house and they let me in and out almost any time I wanted. At first I liked being in all night, but after a while that wore off and I yearned after that "old devil moon," as the saying goes. When the moon came out full, I will admit, it made me wild to be out there with all the night noises, breezes and smells. But that's almost the only important thing that we differed on, Ralph and me. I could sit for hours pointing to the door to no avail, but he absolutely said no to late night roaming. For quite a while, I could fool him; I would go out after dinner and sit on the deck until he lost interest in me and then off I would go, into the wild. Good life!

After a while though, I began to wonder if someone was giving Ralph tips on my psyche. So, when Ralph came out to look for me at sunset, I slipped off the deck and hid in the bushes. It was amusing to be within inches of him, and he still couldn't see me. He walked right past me, looking and calling. Rarely did he spot me, even with his flashlight. But, I digress, back to my psyche: Ralph started bringing my food dish downstairs to entice me in. I tried to ignore him but that "rattle, rattle, rattle" of the food in the dish just couldn't be ignored. I suckered and came in. But it was almost worth giving in to the rattle when I saw how it pleased Ralph to think that he had outsmarted me again. I could have stayed out, and sometimes I did, but I admit, I liked to make Ralph happy.

Of course, there are always problems. Little Feather followed me to my new home; he wanted to stay with me. I didn't have the heart to chase him off, but I could have! Actually, I thought he would go over to live with a recently widowed neighbor after Terry left because that's where he was born and she had said he could come back. I certainly didn't want him and Rachel didn't either. But Little Feather wouldn't leave me. After quite a long time, they gave in and let him live with us. But at least he stayed in the garage, not the house. They renamed him too; they called him Norman Bates.

One day, I was lazily drowsing on the deck when Rachel brought the black fur bag out—big mistake. When it jumped off her lap, Norman Bates jumped on it, and all hell broke loose.

Both of them ran to the end of the deck with Rachel right behind. I don't know how (or why) she did it, but she grabbed the black one by a leg and both cats started biting everything in reach. Of course, I jumped in too;

who would miss fun like that? I'm not sure who bit who, but Rachel came out of the mess holding a hissing, screaming, twisting bag of black fur and I ended up cornering Norman down at the end of the deck while they ran into the house dripping blood. Whoa, did that ever get the old adrenalin pumping, sort of like old times. To this day, Ralph swears that I jumped in to protect Rachel; who's to say I didn't?

I had to work hard to keep my property safe. Once I had to run off a ragged wild cat; Ralph called him "Gruff." I don't know where he came from, but after a day or so of his scouting my property, I jumped him and ran him off. I was sore for about a week after that little tussle. He scouted us for another day or so, but finally he left for good.

And then there was the rattlesnake. I don't know how he crept up on me, but he did. I guess I felt safe on my own property, and the deck seemed so protected that I forgot to keep one eye open. Anyway, one sunny afternoon, I was awakened by a thump on my leg. Luckily I snapped out of my nap quickly and ran it off so I was the only one it struck. All afternoon I stayed under the deck, and when Ralph got home he had to come get me because I just didn't feel like moving. By the next morning it was obvious that I still felt crummy and my leg had swelled up. So off we went to the doctor. He wrapped my leg up like a mummy. It was a long time before I really felt well after that little adventure. I decided to stay away from snakes.

And Norman and I had a few tussles too. As he got more mature, he started feeling his oats, and it was difficult to keep him in control. We left a few cuts and bruises on each other, but for the most part, we lived together carefully, on guard, but peaceful.

As I said before, life was good; the months of good days and nights just blur into one long, warm, blissful, summer afternoon in my mind. I would spend the day drowsing in the sunshine and when they got home from work, Ralph would pick me up, stick his nose into my fur and say, "Ummm, I can smell you've been musking all day." I probably should say, again, that I really did not like being picked up: it's a cat thing. Ralph was different, though, I liked him. But again, I digress. I fell into the family routine. Every Monday through Friday at dusk, their car would pull into the driveway, and since I knew Ralph needed to see me dash up from the back of the house to greet him, what the heck? I needed the exercise. And then on most Fridays, we all got tuna for dinner. Tuna—loved it. Saturday and Sunday we just stayed around the house all day. I tried to sleep inside as much as I could because the house needed lots more color on the furniture—white, that is.

The holidays were full. We had company for Thanksgiving, Christmas and Easter. And, by the way, I want to set the record straight for any of the grandkids who might read my meanderings: I did not lay those Easter eggs. Ralph had a funny sense of humor, but that one was too much. I didn't lay giant candy eggs!

I liked Pine Valley Days best of all because we had a real crowd of people and they stayed for several days. And second, Thanksgiving; but then maybe Christmas was best, but then again, maybe it was Easter; I just can't decide. It was fun whenever the family came because of the commotion and food. There was always someone around who wanted to stroke me and feed me. I could pull my "drop, thump" trick and it never failed to get me a good scratch.

There are some humans who don't need much attention. Rachel was that way, but Ralph, he's a whole different person. I knew my mission was to follow him around all day long to keep him happy. If he got up and went to the kitchen, I'd follow; if he got up and went to the bedroom, I'd follow; if he got up and went outside, I'd follow. Sometimes it tired me, but I did feel it was my job to keep him company. Of course, there were perks for me; he was always good for a scratch, a belly rub and a deep chuckle.

My very favorite interval was our personal cleansing routine. Every morning after breakfast, all three of us would head down the hallway to the bedroom. I took my place right in front of the bathroom cabinets, curled up and went to sleep. By the time I woke up they were all showered, shaved, brushed, dressed and ready to start their day. That was when the fun started for me, err, Ralph: Ralph would shoo Rachel out and lay down with me and scratch, rub and sooth until my front paws curled. I would purr so loud for him that it almost made me laugh at his pleasure. It did feel good, and the togetherness was something that Ralph needed. I knew it took all my encouragement and help to get his day started right.

But then again, maybe my very favorite time of day was our evening ritual. After Rachel went to bed, Ralph would go into the living room and stand very still for a long time, while I sat at his feet. I don't quite know why, or what he was doing, but there was something mystical about that session; curiously I always felt better afterward. Then he would sit down in his chair, which was my signal to jump up. We would spend several minutes just scratching and rubbing and communing. Ralph needed this time together, and of course, I was never one to turn down a good scratch. This quiet evening time with Ralph was, in some strange way, solace for my soul.

Remember I started this story, way back, by saying that I had a "feeling" about Ralph? Well, maybe I did, I don't know. I think I did, but I knew the time had come; my mission with Ralph was complete. We had quite a few good years and I did a good job. In return, he gave me a life that was just about as good as it gets. I guess this is as good a time as any to repeat, "There are always problems." And, as I mentioned earlier, I did have a doctor. Remember, I said he called me Ear Pie? My veterinarian and his nurse were another good happening in my life. Nurse was always good for scratches, and my doctor was another human who, like Ralph, gave off good vibes. Unfortunately, they appeared in my life at a time that wasn't much fun. They tried, they really did, but with no success. When I do a thing, I do it good (or bad as it turned out). And that "thing," along with my feeling that my work with Ralph was complete, helped me make a big decision: as good as life was with my family, after all the years we spent together, and in spite of the ideal existence that I had carved, I knew it was time to go, to start another life; it's a cat thing. And remember, I still have eight more lives to go. So I left home. As a general rule, we cats can flip our tails, go, and not look back, but not this time; I still keep my eye on Ralph. I see him out on our deck almost every morning and I know he's looking. Well, so am I, I see him; I see him.

Epilogue

Life here in Heaven is good, but in the first week of September 2006, I got that feeling again, you know, that "Ralph" feeling.

I started walking. The longer I walked, the stronger the feeling. Within an hour the feeling was forceful enough that I knew I was tracking. I stopped and looked around. And there he was.

I saw him at the exact moment he saw me; the joy in my heart was equal to the joy I saw on his face. By now you all know that I'm one tough guy. I'm cool. I don't run for anyone, but I started running. The Big Guy that lives here in Heaven shines joy on the entire world, so don't get me wrong, I'm not comparing the two, but in the world of humans, Ralph is just "It" for me. He was surrounded by family and friends, but he left his circle of humans and scooped me up before I could greet him with my drop, thump trick.

Now don't get me wrong, I've loved my life here: good food, plenty of warm sun spots, bees, insects and birds; even my twin sister to pal around with again. And to be truthful, I didn't even know I'd missed Ralph until I got that feeling. That's how the Big Guy works it, you know: total contentment. So I can't say I missed Ralph because I didn't. He wasn't physically here, but in some way he was with me. I know that sounds confusing but it's true.

So now I live with Ralph again, we jog together, well, he jogs, I walk, then we sit in the sun and bask for hours at a time. It's a good life we have. However, when I see him go still for long periods of time, see him looking off into space. I know he's watching over his earthly people. I did that too, so I know. But before he can blink his eyes, they'll all be here with us.

THE LIBERATED
FELINE

It's okay to be fat. So you're fat. Just be fat & shut up about it.

—ROSEANNE BARR

Proud Me

The little black kitten had grown up. Really, really UP and OUT. And she was very sensitive about her body.

When life started for her, she was tiny and furry. Her first days are not part of her memory bank. Most beings' earliest memories are of a particularly sweet, sad, unpleasant or traumatic occurrence. Boots was no different. She faintly recalls being very hungry, very thirsty and very frightened. Something was tangled around her body and she could barely move. She was so exhausted that sleep was the most inviting thought she could dredge up. She was going to sleep.

But something miraculous happened. A tall human brought her cool water and untangled her from the hated bindings. But he left, and she knew she would become tangled again, she just knew it. The hated binding was still connected to her.

And sure enough, slowly the tangles started, and every time she moved they became tighter and tighter until she sadly dropped to the hot cement floor and tried to sleep forever.

And again, the tall human came to her. This time he took the hated binding off completely and gently put her into a soft spot. And that's the beginning of her life's memory bank.

After The Happening, Boots started to grow, to learn, to play and to eat. She grew from tiny to large to larger, and her fur turned shiny and beautiful.

She had a huge new world to explore. There were smells that were so exquisite they made her sinuses hurt. There were butterflies, bugs, bees, flies and dirt—lovely, warm dirt to roll in. There was all the water a kitten could drink, so she often played with it, trying to bat it with her paws, but water turned out to be sort of tricky and hard to catch. And she had a bowl of food that never emptied. Throughout her days of running, climbing, scratching and sleeping, she would dash to her bowl of food and it never emptied. No matter how much she ate, it was always filled, like magic.

There was one flaw in her new life. She wasn't the only cat living in her world. Norman Bates was an ugly, striped garage cat who lived right outside her door. He didn't come inside often but when he did, Boots had to protect her world, and the fur flew. When she went outside, Norman wouldn't leave her alone. He insisted on sticking his nose in her face. And again, the fur would fly.

After a while, Boots stopped going out much. Norman had a voice that was hard to bear, so she kept as far away from him as possible. She only ventured outside when the humans went with her. They kept the unpleasant, intolerable Norman Bates busy.

As time passed, Boots and Norman Bates came to an understanding. She had the house and he had the outside and garage. Time dulled their angst toward each other and life together became relatively peaceful.

Norman, however, had an unfortunate habit. He knew his voice was irritating, so when he came into Boots' realm, he always managed to say something to upset her. He worked hard at it. One would think that this small problem was bearable, but to Boots, an encounter with Norman was enough to keep her awake and prowling the halls at night. He was the one blotch in her world. She tried to avoid his existence.

When Norman and Boots did come within nosing reach, she tried to be polite and dignified. Norman, however, made his awkward attempts at jocularity. As he was socially inept, he never learned to leave her alone. Often his remarks put her in a foul mood for days. Still, she was a lady and didn't respond with hisses and spitting as she would have liked.

But life was good. The good days blended into weeks and months and years until one morning when Boots tried to leap up onto the couch. She couldn't. What a shock!

She sat down on the carpet and thought about it. And the more she thought, the more she realized this was not a new problem. It had been slowly creeping up on her.

She had been having difficulties for some time. Just last night, she wanted to leap onto the bed, but even thinking about it was too much trouble, so she curled up on the carpet and went to sleep.

As she thought, she realized there were other problems. She could no longer reach every part of her body during her cleaning sessions. And her hind legs were achy much of the time. Was this a normal part of aging? But as Boots toured her house looking out all the windows at her neighborhood, she saw cats of many different ages, and they all leaped. Why, just last week she had seen the cat that lived across the street leap up and grab a passing bird; made a mess of it, too. And Norman Bates, who was older than Boots, was always dashing around the yard catching lizards. He ate their tails, ugh. Of course it didn't take leaping to catch a lizard, but out of curiosity, Boots took off running and pretended to catch a lizard.

Oops! That was a sobering experience. She couldn't run, either.

So, she couldn't leap anymore, she couldn't run anymore, she couldn't reach all of her body parts, and finally, her hind legs were stiff. She had a problem. As she thought about her problem, she realized there were times when the sight of her food bowl made her nauseous, sort of like she had maybe eaten too much.

As Boots gazed out the window, she slowly realized something. The other cats were sleek and furry. They weren't plump and furry. But she was. She thought and thought, and finally the notion came to her that maybe she was eating too much. She was fat. Fat, fat, fat! What to do? All day long and all night long, Boots pondered her problem. She came to the conclusion that she would have to go on a diet. It was a horrid word, diet. Boots' wonderful world was wonderful, in great part, because her food bowl was always full. Since she had come to live in this house she had never, not once, encountered an empty bowl. What a dilemma!

And this puts us right back to the beginning of this little story: The little black kitten had grown up. Really, really UP and OUT! And she was becoming very sensitive about her body.

Alright, it couldn't be helped. She would cut her trips to her food bowl in half. And she would make it a point to run up and down the hallway at least three times a day. That should do it. And soon she would be sleek again. She would.

Well, as females the world over have learned as long as females have been in existence, it isn't easy to lose weight. And exercising is tiring. If you don't eat, you get tired. And if you're tired, you can't exercise. It's a vicious circle. So Boots tried and tried. And as the days passed and the weeks passed, she tried. But there were no results.

She wandered her house daily, mourning her sleek, youthful body. And as she wandered, she felt her pudginess. She began to dodge out of sight when Norman Bates passed by the windows. She just knew he would say something to irritate her. She would keep out of sight until she was sleek again.

Diet, diet, diet. It was on her mind day and night. She would wander into her dining room and nibble half a bowl of food before she realized what she was doing. She would go for a drink of fresh water and before she knew it she had, again, nibbled from her food. Her life was made a living hell because there was no escaping her problem. It was with her 24/7.

Then one sunny day when her humans invited her out onto the deck she ran into Norman Bates. As always, he had much to say in his loud, irritating voice. Boots, in her most dignified way, walked away from him. Mistake! Norman looked at her and swung his head for a second look. "Hey," he said. "You expecting kittens? How? I haven't seen any Toms around here." Mortified, Boots scuttled into the house as fast as she could. But she burned.

After that day, Boots imagined that Norman was looking at her every time she went near the windows. Life was miserable. So she ate. And she moped. And life wasn't good.

But Boots was a proud cat with a buoyant personality, and she decided she would not live this way. Yes, she was pudgy. Fat, if you will. But Norman Bates was the last cat on earth that should have any reason to feel superior to her. Fat! Harrumph. Norman had bad breath; his fur was skimpy and fell out in clumps; and his voice sounded like a warped bagpipe. Who was he to judge beauty? That very evening, when Norman Bates came to the door for his dinner, Boots was waiting defiantly. When he walked across the threshold, he attempted to stick his nose on Boots' nose but, of course, she backed away. Norman started in. "Have you had your dinner yet? Oh, sorry, looks like you've already eaten—lots." Snicker, snicker.

Ms. Boots drew her plump furry body up as tight as it would go and, in a dignified voice, said to the unbearable Mr. Bates, "I know I'm not abstemious in my diet, but your being facetious is just plain rude."

Mr. Bates' face dropped and he was left with the only thing he could think to say, "Huh? W'ad she say? W'ad she say about my abs? W'at's wrong with my face?"

The newly liberated Ms. Boots swished her lovely, fluffy tail, turned her plump, well, fat body, and marched away triumphantly.

No more diet, no more wailing and moaning, and no more training for a noxious 10K, either. Once again, life was good for Ms. Two Boots Costantino.

TWO WEEKS OUT OF TIME

Whether we're prepared or not,
life has a habit of thrusting situations upon us.

—LUCILLE BALL

Survival

Passing Time

Uh, damn! Can't see ... Can't hear ... Where am I? Sound-proof room? Curious. Can't move ... Dreaming, that's it ... Dream won't go away ... Floatin' ... Floatin' ... Not a dream, nightmare ... Too dark ... CAN'T WAKE UP! ... Why? Ugh, ah, man, does this hurt. Dream won't go away. Hurts so much ... Can't see, can't hear, and can't move. Hurts like hell ... What? Oh ... hear somethin', but too far ... Guys from work? A joke? But the pain. Really them? Strange. Yeah, really is them, know their voices. Why don't they help me?

Back to Reality

Where'd the guys go? Now it's my girls and my sister. And my mom, I hear her voice. My brother? My niece? Yeah, it is them. Odd, so far away; gettin' closer now. Hey, I can feel 'em. Touchin' me, but soft, hardly a touch, odd. Man, I hurt. Wake up, wake up! Don't like this. Nightmare ... Not dead, too much pain ... I can see! I'm not blind, but man, this is scary. Where am I? My girls are here again. I see 'em. I hear 'em. Not talkin' to me though. Funny. No, not funny. They said accident? Hospital? Not dreamin' … Real? Doctors? Yeah, gotta be, they're all in white. Why am I so confused?

Where? … Not here anymore … Oh, yeah, they are … Feel someone; so soft, touchin' me, weird. Wake up! Wake up!

Think, think, okay, hospital. How'd I get here? How long? Why? I hear 'em but they don't seem to know it. Do they think I'm dead?

I see, I hear but no one knows it. Why can't they see my eyes are open? Why don't they know? I feel but can't move. I think but can't talk.

Time just goes on and on and on. Is it day or night? They're always here. My brother-in-law, too. Can't tell day from night. Sometimes they're all here and sometimes only some of them. Doesn't this place have visiting hours? How did my oldest girl get here? She lives so far away. Maybe I am dyin'.

They're talkin'. Okay, heard that. Damaged my brain? Whoa, that's a thought. Don't feel like a cabbage. They're wrong, I'm still in here. Can't move though, maybe paralyzed. Still have legs, feel 'em movin'. Maybe not though, maybe I only think they're movin'. Wish I knew. Wish I could remember.

On my bike; that's the last thing I remember. That's gotta be bad because if that's the last thing I remember, I must've plowed into something. I must have! Think! Think! Why can't I remember?

I'm flyin' through the air like an eagle. I can feel it. I'm free. My hands control the bike like it's part of me. My legs are holdin' on to the bike strong. Free from everything, no worries, no nothin'; just the wind in my face and, man, I'm feeling' good. What happened?

Uh, uh, owww, that one hurt, but at least I'm feeling. That's my damn hand and that's my damn chest. Awww, it hurts ... I sure as hell have a stomach because it HURTS! How long can this go on?

Yeah, it hurts bad, but not as bad as not knowin' what's goin' on! Awww, owww, what are they doin' and why are they doin' it? Wish I could make em' stop. Just leave me alone!

Ahhh, that's better ... aw, no, they're at it again; they're pickin' me up! Aghh, that hurrrrrts! Now I'm movin', what the hell? Where are they takin' me? Okay, okay, don't panic. I'm in a hospital. And I'm bein' rolled somewhere, surgery, x-rays, somethin'. Yeah, that's gotta be it. Phew, I won't survive much more of this. They'll kill me. Sheeeeit; now I know why Pop hated hospitals. I don't like this. JUST LEAVE ME ALONE! I swear, I'll heal myself ... God help me! Lord, give me strength! Help me! Help me!

CHEERIO TEARS

… Why should I be out of mind because I am out of sight? …

—HENRY SCOTT HOLLAND

Prologue

This is a story of Floyd Oscar Burris, Jr., born on December 14, 1942. Written for my granddaughters, this is a story of my brother, your great uncle. Every word is true.

Chapter One

Floyd Oscar Burris, Junior, was born on December 14, 1942. That was a long, long time ago. He had an older brother. And he had an older sister.

When Junior's father woke Sister in the middle of the night to report Junior's birth, she had a small temper tantrum; she didn't want another brother. She needed a sister! After she saw him for the first time, though, she was never again unhappy with her baby brother. He was perfect.

Some nights he kept the whole family awake with his crying, but Sister had earaches that kept the whole family awake, so she couldn't very well complain about his tummy ache, could she? And anyway, by morning he was always smiling and happy again.

Junior had dimples in both cheeks, large brown eyes, and his brown hair fell into curls over his forehead.

Chapter Two

Brother and Sister argued about almost everything. If Sister was told to wash the dishes after dinner while Brother was to dry the dishes, Sister knew that the dishes tonight were much dirtier than last night when Brother got to wash. By the way, did you know that when these children were small, there were no dishwashers? Children all over the country washed and dried dinner dishes by hand. Brother and Sister argued about this constantly. But on one subject alone, they agreed: Junior was the most beautiful, most lovable little brother that had ever been born. This they knew.

Sister had just started school when Junior was born, and she was allowed to take Junior to school to "share" him with her classmates. Sister also loved to share stories of his mischief with her classmates. And when there was no real Junior mischief to report, Sister was often guilty of making up a story, just because she liked talking about him. Sister's teacher understood the importance of this wonderful possession of Sister's—her baby brother—for he was Sister's. She claimed him as her very own; she "allowed" her family to enjoy him, but he belonged to Sister.

Chapter Three

As Junior grew from toddler to little boy, he had two friends, Johnny and Billy. Johnny was tall, with a dimple in his chin, was quiet and almost exactly the same age as Junior. Billy was short, had long, curly, blond hair, a constant smile and was younger by a year than the other two. The three little boys were together as much as afternoon naps and mothers would allow. From morning to night, they played together in the dirt, on the grass, with toy trucks, and with toy cars, in front yards and back. Their three homes were all close together on a quiet cul-de-sac, with almost no traffic for mothers to be concerned with. The three little boys were free to roam their neighborhood with little supervision. This was the 1940s and it was safe for children to play outside unattended.

For one whole, warm summer when the boys were five and six years old, they wore only swimsuits all summer long, from morning to night. Junior's little body turned browner and browner by the day. His mother had started to teach him to bathe himself. He would be starting school in September, so he had to learn these grownup tasks. One day, toward the end of summer, a shopping trip was planned for school clothes. Junior's mother was in a hurry and he needed a bath. So rather than leave Junior to his usual dawdling in the bathtub, she started to scrub him. The more she scrubbed, the whiter he became. All summer long, she thought Junior was getting tanned from being in the sun all day wearing only his little swimsuit. Not so. Junior's little body was just plain dirty; he was brown with dirt. His mother never, ever got over the embarrassment of that summer discovery. By the way, Junior's mother was your great grandmother Burris.

Chapter Four

Junior loved Cheerios for breakfast, he loved Cheerios for lunch. He just loved Cheerios. They created much happiness in Junior's life, Cheerios did.

Junior was a very happy little boy and easy to please. There came a morning, though, when he tried to pour his Cheerios out into the cereal bowl and there was nothing. The box was empty. As Sister watched, his little face was etched into her memory; he said nothing, he demanded nothing, he simply sat at the table in great sorrow with tears in his eyes. No sound; just one huge tear swimming in each eye.

There was no family car, so within minutes, Sister was walking out the door on her way to the store for Cheerios. It was a twenty minute walk each way, but she was happy to go. Usually, Sister would be grumpy and annoyed at having to go to the store; however, her baby brother was sad, so this time, walking to the store was not a burden.

Chapter Five

From the time he was able to understand words, Little Golden Books were read to Junior. First Mother read to him, then Brother and Sister. He sat quietly for as long as someone would read to him and when they tired, there was no tantrum, he simply took his books and sat quietly, flipping through the pages.

Junior's favorites were "The Little Engine That Could" and "The Pokey Little Puppy." He would carry these little books around with him, sit down wherever an adult or brother or sister sat, and wait. He might lean on their leg to remind them of his presence, but he never had to wait long because his quiet company was inviting. Perhaps if he had nagged or demanded, his family wouldn't have been so ready to drop everything for him, but he didn't; he just sat patiently and waited to be noticed. Of course, occasionally someone would be out of sorts, and there may have been times when he was refused, but if so, he would quietly find someone else.

Chapter Six

Pancho lived with Junior. Pancho was his dog, a completely black dog. There may have been some white on him somewhere, but I can't remember where it would have been. He slept with Junior and where Junior went, Pancho was sure to follow closely. When Junior was old enough to start school, Pancho stayed home and waited for him. He slept at the end of the sidewalk, waiting patiently.

When the family was at dinner, Pancho could be found sitting under the table, watching for whatever might be handed to him. There were three children sitting at the dinner table; three small sets of hands to silently slip pieces of meat down to Pancho. Pancho was very well fed.

Epilogue

Junior was your great uncle. He grew into a very handsome young man. He married while very young, had four children, and died when he was only twenty-five years old, but he isn't forgotten.

UNFINISHED

I am I, and you are you.
Whatever we were to each other,
that we still are.

—HENRY SCOTT HOLLAND

Gone

A telephone ringing in the early morning hours is an eerie, ominous sound. Anyone who's lived long enough to go through a tragedy knows that bad news always comes in the early morning hours through a telephone call. When the ringing woke me, I knew it wasn't good, but not this. Not this. I picked up the phone, listened, returned it to its base, crawled back under the covers shivering and lay there silently. My husband reached out and gently touched me, asking, "Who was that?" "My brother's dead," was my whisper. "Junior's dead."

The church was in Pacific Beach but even now, thirty years later, I could not lead you to it. We drove to the services in our own car, knowing it would be simpler to navigate throughout the day if we had our own transportation. It was a good choice because we had three children to look after and neither my husband nor I were functioning well. Floyd Jr. was dead. How could that be? Yes, I knew the facts: his car had hit a concrete wall abutting a bridge and he didn't survive the impact. But that didn't explain to my soul how it could be that I no longer had a little brother. I sat through the services with uncontrolled trembling; I heard the words, I saw my family and friends in their sorrow. No words, nothing, could help the chaos in my head. How to conduct the rest of my life knowing that he was no longer here? My grief was so deep that I had to deliberate on each movement I made. I was thirty years old when he died and today I am sixty-seven; as irrational as it may seem now, it is truth to say I was so disoriented I barely knew who I was: if my brother was gone, and if I was no longer a sister to Junior, then who was I? Again, it sounds absurd, but I had to think carefully to know which body part to move to gain a specific outcome; nothing followed automatically. The loss was so enormous that when he was removed from my life, I was shaken to my core.

Who was this man? What about him gripped my life so fiercely that when he was removed I was left unwhole? I had a full life, a loving husband and three wonderful children, but I was lost when he died.

Floyd, Jr. was twenty-five years old, he had been married, he had four children, he had earned a Bachelor's degree in Chemistry and the world had been laid out before him. But he was gone.

I REMEMBER

... for she was set apart for you before the world existed.

—TOBIT 6:18

Fifty-Four Years

Let me tell you a love story. This love story is a rare one in these times of "make me happy, damn it, right now," and the young people of today are the losers. From 1952 to this day in 2006, I have loved one man desperately. Everything in me loves him. My whole soul and being is his. I've adored him, I've worshipped him, I've needed him, I've admired him, I've pitied him, I've been very angry with him, but most of all, through all the years, I've simply loved him. He filled my every need to the extent that I have no doubt that I was born and he was born—each for the other. That it was God's plan is the only way to explain the fact that we found each other at such a tender age and were committed for life from the very beginning.

Our love story is winding down. I watch him and I know it deep in my soul.

I remember him. I remember the first time I ever saw him. He was standing with a group of kids on the high school cafeteria porch. His thick, black, curly hair surrounded the most beautiful face I had ever seen on a guy. He was grinning at me with a lopsided grin. I was to discover that he actually is sort of lopsided; his lips are irregular and one shoulder is higher than the other. He was wearing a brown leather bomber jacket, a white shirt, Levis and yes, blue suede shoes. As he grinned at me, I noticed how slim he was, and his legs seemed to be longer than normal for his height, and his feet were really, really big. All these years later, with the haze of time filming my memories, I still see him with his head tipped back, grinning at me.

My friend Ann beckoned to me, so I walked over to them. She introduced us and after giggling nervously for a minute or two, I left. That was the beginning of the rest of my life.

There were other things on my mind. My current interest was Cisco, a guy who was a notorious flirt. Actually, my dad had decreed that there would be no dating until I turned sixteen. It was fall of 1951, I was in the 9th grade, and I was fourteen and a half years old.

By the time I had gone through Cisco and at least four or five other guys, it was 1952 and almost time for school to let out for the summer. I had been aware of him throughout the school year because every time I turned around, he was on the scene watching me: at school, walking home from school, at the shopping center sitting on the back of a bench. It was a bit embarrassing because when I walked by him, I had to stop and talk to him or appear to be a snoot. But I had nothing to say to him. My attention was tuned to the popular guys: Bobby, Tommy, Wayne and Mike.

His presence slowly intruded into my subconscious. All through the months from late 1951 until June 1952, his interest never wavered. No matter how I ignored, teased or insulted him, he was still there, just around the corner. He was a senior and getting ready to graduate, but I said no when he asked me to go out with him on graduation night. That hurt him, yet still he stayed, always nearby.

One morning, after school let out for summer, I realized I hadn't heard from or about him in more than a week—curious. I didn't like not knowing about him—curious. I didn't like not seeing him—curious. I called Ann and asked if she knew where he was. She didn't, but she said to come on over and she would try to find him.

That night, Ann invited several other girls and guys for a party and he and I were paired. It was a new experience because he was so intense. All my adventures with boys had been giggling, fidgeting and holding hands, and that was about it. This was something new. This guy wanted something from me and I didn't even know what it was. He touched me inside my head and somehow, I knew this was important. I had just turned fifteen. How should I deal with this human being who just wanted to love me? How did I know this was love? I can't say. What I am prepared to say is that it felt right. He smelled like Old Spice aftershave and freshly ironed clothes. He was warm and protective. More than that, we seemed to fit; he felt like the other half of me. I felt as though my entire life had been spent in preparation for my melding with this one person.

His was a heavy presence. I say heavy because he wanted so much. He wanted all of me, and I only knew how to hold hands with boys. And when I say "all of me," I didn't even know what that meant. Remember, I was just barely fifteen years old and after all, it was 1952, not 2006. I only knew he wanted to absorb me. Was I ready for that? And how could I walk away from him after promising him so much on that first evening? And how could I walk away from him when he fit into my head with such precision? The wholeness of my feeling about him was so right.

His graduation present from his parents had been a car. If you ever listened to him on the subject of how he finally caught my interest, he would say, "It was the car. She wouldn't have anything to do with me until I got the car."

And that's how it began. As I write, the memory of his arms around me warms me still. The scent of him brings pleasure to me still. The sound of his voice still brings me alive. And after all this time, I do remember how it felt to be in love for the first time; really in love.

The memories flood in. We were young, in love, and so happy. Everything is rich when you're young and in love. The sun shines brighter on your face, wind excites your skin, rain is softer and music is unbearably intense. The touch of another human being is more exquisite than mere words can describe. Feelings are so rich as to be excruciating. Oh, yes, I remember.

When I watch him now, I see him as he is but I also see him as he was. The two visions blend so that I never know which man will turn around to see me watching. He's seventy-one now, but he's also seventeen.

That first summer was glorious. My whole world revolved around him. After we started going together, I had no other interests. High school and the next three years were simply years to live through. Since I was only fifteen and marriage wasn't a possibility until I was eighteen and graduated from high school, this was a period suspended in time. I knew that nothing important was going to happen until our marriage. All this occurred before I was allowed to date openly. My no-dating problem still existed, but now that he had his graduation present (a 1942, yellow and brown Chevy Coupe), nothing could keep us apart. We were mobile. His job at Convair was time-consuming, but he wasn't very good at going to work that summer. And, of course, my dad had no inkling of what was going on in his midst. We spent one whole year dodging my dad.

By 1953, and my sixteenth birthday, the atmosphere between my dad and me was armed warfare. There was no friendliness at all. I wanted to be free to date and my dad wanted to protect me. Of course there was a blowup. When the dust settled, I was finally free to date.

But my Oklahoma-born father didn't count on my bringing home a Mexican/Italian. Uh oh! That wasn't going to work. The armed warfare flared again with an even more explosive blowup. Again I won. I could bring him home and date him freely.

My Dad learned to like him, to love him, to respect him and to admire him. And I was thrilled with his family, all of them. To this day I wear his Italian grandmother's engagement ring as my own. The two years between 1953 and 1955 flew by, and the wedding my parents gave us was as grand a wedding as we could imagine.

Our life blew past us like the wind. We bought our first home. We blinked and three years of marriage were gone, and we were ready to start a family. Within three more years, we were the parents of David Ralph, Damon Carlo and Kathleen Marie. We were a family and all our dreams had come true.

Life was harder with three children because the time simply wasn't there to do justice to each child and a mate too. Somehow our marriage didn't suffer much. I remember being torn in two directions, but I also remember the exhilaration of living the dream of my life. I was exactly where I had always wanted to be. I was a wife and I was a mother. But this isn't a story of family. Our three children grew up to be powerful, strong, productive and admirable people, and just saying they were fun says nothing. They were, and are, a world of love, joy and satisfaction. But their story and our life with them is a whole 'nother story; this is just of him.

His strength of will was legendary. He was in his late twenties. He had been a jogger all our married life. Long before it became trendy to jog, he ran and ran and ran. At Convair, he worked with someone who played basketball. It became a running joke between the two of them as to which one had more endurance. Finally, there came a showdown. They met on a nearby high school track on a Saturday morning. The rules were that whoever could run one-half mile further than the other was the winner. He ran seven miles before the other man dropped from exhaustion and he ran one-half mile further before he allowed himself to stop. He had never run more than three or four miles until that Saturday morning. He thought he was going to die on the track, but it wasn't in him to stop. He would say later, when retelling the story, that just before the other fellow dropped, his own chest throbbed so heavily he thought he was having a heart attack. Even so, he knew he would win; he just didn't know how long he would have to run to do it. As long as I've known him, that's been his approach to any problem. He will not quit.

Remember my dad? My dad who fought so hard to keep us apart? Well, he was an alcoholic; a long time, happy drunk. And when my dad's and my mother's life began to unravel because of his drinking, there came a time when a residential move had to be made that my dad didn't want. It was necessary that we help my mother and brother make the move while my dad spent the whole day rambling and interfering in the hard work of the move. Late that night, we got a call from my mother that my dad was back in the old neighborhood scaring the neighbors. So my guy and my brother took off to round up my dad. When they got to the house, sure enough, my dad was there, sitting on the porch, drinking. After trying for some time to convince him to come peacefully, the two younger men got my dad to the station wagon (remember station wagons?) only to get him no further. He would not be cajoled into the vehicle; it was going to take force. So my guy told my brother to move back, that things might get rough and he didn't want a son to have to manhandle his father. My dad heard this and immediately got irritated, saying, "Oh, ho, you think you can take me? I don't think so."

Well, it did get a bit rough. My guy physically picked my dad up and dumped him into the back of the station wagon, the back was slammed shut and locked, and the three men started for home. My dad slumbered peacefully for a while. At some point during the drive home, my dad woke up and started laughing. With one eye on my guy and the other eye closed, he said, "You're pretty smart, aren't you? You got me," and they laughed about it all the way home. They were still friends, and my brother never had to use force on his father. That's my guy, my hero.

Life became more of an adventure when he decided to go to college. It's a bit difficult for a man with a wife and three kids to make that decision. His grandparents and parents supported us for the next six years. How many families do you know that would opt for that plan? His family encouraged it and for the first time, we dreamed of an objective higher than Convair. After junior college, he transferred to what was then called San Diego State College. Now it's San Diego State University (SDSU). College studies weren't difficult for him. He spent most of his study time at home. To cut down on expenses, we garaged our car and he bought a Honda Scrambler motorcycle, and for the first time I had real competition for his attention because he loved that Scrambler. He had something done to the engine that made it a real "hot" machine. I can still close my eyes and see him doing "wheelies" on that Scrambler.

Our idyllic life didn't last, for in late summer of 1967, before he was to start his last semester at State College, he was diagnosed with a deadly cancer. The devastation I knew in the following weeks was so complete that I barely remember living. Life was suspended. I don't remember caring for my children. I must have readied them for school. I must have cooked meals. I must have cleaned house. I remember nothing of the trivialities of life, but I do remember the time spent with him. He insisted that we only speak positively. He insisted we "keep the balloon up in the air." Keep laughing ... keep living

... hard to do ... but he did it. Through all the radiation and surgeries—for there were more—and resulting sicknesses, he kept our whole family together. For the rest of his life, he lived with pain caused from the radiation. But he lived.

At some point, he finally sold his beloved Scrambler, not because he felt he wouldn't live, for he insisted that he would live, but because of finances. His parents had shouldered the entire burden of his education and the medical bills were sky-high; the bike had to go. To this day, he listens, watches, and smiles when he hears the distinctive sound of a Honda Scrambler.

He didn't complain. His loud affirmation of his life was that he had had the best life of anyone he had ever known and he wouldn't trade away one minute of his pain if it meant giving up any of the people in his life. Anything was worth the life that he was given and the people in his world ... Courageous? I think so.

He finished college and went on to University of San Diego Law School. Law school wasn't easy for him (he hated it), but he graduated, took the bar examination and failed, then took it again and passed. In January of 1974, having been in only two law offices in his entire life, he set out to build a law practice.

Through the harsh years of illness and law school, I loved him even more, and my admiration grew so that he became a giant to me. Law school was very hard on his ego because he was older than most of the other students and he was in over his head for the whole three years. He didn't understand much of what he was called on to study. But he did it. He came near to withdrawing but didn't. He found the strength from within, and it was always his constant refrain that God never gave him more than he could handle; he was never left alone. God was with him always.

While he was establishing himself in law, he taught business law at Grossmont College, and he taught a class for legal secretaries at Coleman College. He rarely had a day without abdominal pain or discomfort of some kind. More nights than I can number, he spent writhing in pain, and in the morning he would go off to Coleman College to teach his class of future legal secretaries. He told me of one such morning when he was so dizzy and tired that he stopped at a telephone pole just to hang on to something. Several of his students passed him by and stopped to ask if they could help. He must have looked like he was just coming in after an all-night binge.

There should be no sickness in a love story, but how to tell a glorious story and leave out the pain? And how did we get to be forty? The last time I looked we were thirty.

After the cancer came vitiligo. Those of you who knew him in his early years will remember his dark skin. That dark skin turned to splotchy, then to white over a period of years, but it wasn't quick and it wasn't easy. I watched him go through all the stages of vitiligo, each new one worse than the last, until his skin was no longer brown but a pale white. There was nothing anyone could do. But I did find myself moving to him to grasp his hand or arm when a child's scrutiny became too intense, as if my touching him would let the gawking child know this man was loved. And he was loved. He was loved.

He had been practicing law for about seven years when I started working with him as his secretary. It wasn't our plan for me to stay more than a couple of months, but I found that I loved his business. His clients were interesting and their problems were intriguing. I gained a whole new respect for the depth of this man I so loved. I watched as he struggled to overcome the misery of his body and plunge himself into the problems of his clients. I learned anew how precise, quirky and unconventional his mind was. I watched in amazement as time after time he picked out a cohesive fact pattern from a smudgy knot and took a winning case to court.

His clients weren't just people who walked through the door. He took on their problems as his own; he took them to bed with us; he tossed and turned with their problems through the night. His tenacity wouldn't permit him to stop until he had facts that favored his client; his trials were with us twenty-four hours a day. As he gained experience, his losses in court were limited. There were losses, of course, but as the years passed, they were few.

Spending twenty-four hours a day with someone is a sure way to learn his every weakness. Instead, I learned more of his strengths. He became bigger than life to me. When we met in high school, he couldn't put together a written sentence. Now the tables were turned and I couldn't understand the sentences he put together. In the first months I worked with him, I typed many of his letters, documents, agreements and court filings without knowing their meaning. He was interesting, funny, congenial, and fascinating, and I was dazzled. What was even more surprising was that I became hooked on his clients; I loved them all.

We almost never ran out of topics of conversation. I can't tell you the number of times we overshot a freeway exit or drove many blocks out of our way because we were absorbed in the subject at hand. It was a good life.

He was proud that he came from the streets of Logan Heights and Linda Vista long before he went to law school. He was proud that he had seen life as an uneducated adult before going to college and on to law school. Having seen the adult world first through uneducated eyes and then through educated eyes, he knew how privileged he was. He was extremely proud that he could drive through Logan Heights and give the "Logan Heights Nod" to the local toughs and get the appropriate responsive nod; it tickled his inner man. And he was proud that he could "swim with the sharks." And yes, he did refer to his legal brethren as sharks. I'm not sure that he would ever have retired if his body hadn't failed him. He loved his life as a lawyer.

We passed from forty to fifty to sixty and beyond. Our bodies faltered and we no longer had the youthful firmness that for so long we had taken for granted. But the soul's heart never falters. After fifty-four years, his voice still pleasures me. After fifty-four years, the light shines brighter when he comes into a room. After fifty-four years, his touch is warm and strengthening. And after fifty-four years, the sound of his voice is the last thing I want to hear as I drift off to sleep.

Congestive heart failure was really the beginning of the end, but he didn't know it. I expected the worst because once again, I went to the books and the Internet. The statistics say that fifty percent live past five years. Once again, he promised me that he would survive. I don't think so. It's been four years since the diagnosis and it doesn't look good.

Our years, our love, passed through many twists and turns. Beginning with the thrill of our new excitement and passion, to comfort, even anger and pain (but never betrayal), and finally, to the curiosity and destruction of old age. We laughed our way through all the years of our lives. We were consumed, and our love lasted two lifetimes, his and mine. He put me on his shoulders when I was fifteen years old and he carried me on his shoulders even when life got heavy (and I got heavier yet) and he never put me down. It's been my honor to share the life of this grand human being, Ralph Salvatore Costantino, my husband, my passion, my lifelong love.

GRANNY, MAGGIE MAE AND SHADRACH

The sound of birds stops the noise in my mind.

—CARLY SIMON

Love Birds

Granny had worked out her schedule to perfection. She got up at 5:30 a.m., which gave her time to leisurely have a cup or two of coffee while answering all her e-mail correspondents, straightening up any clutter she had created the night before, feeding her two cats and cleaning their litter boxes. When all these tasks were completed, she still had time to shower, dress and leave for work at a reasonable time to arrive by 9:00 a.m.

That was before she had the creative idea of bringing a Peach Faced Love Bird into her home. The thought came to her one afternoon while visiting her daughter that a Love Bird would be a cheerful addition to her menagerie. She didn't jump helter-skelter into the project. Instead, she pondered it thoroughly.

For four years her daughter's home had been brightened by two little green Love Birds. They were called "the Boys."

This was a misunderstanding, though, of one of the little birds' gender. Three months ago the family had noticed that the two little birds were busily shredding the paper that covered the bottom of their cage. So frenzied were they in their mission that someone remarked, "Those birds are piling up that shredded paper to look like a nest. Do you suppose they're mating?" The ready answer was, "Nope, that's just the Boys having fun." Sure enough, it wasn't long before one very small egg made an appearance right in the middle of the pile of shredded paper. The surprised family immediately provided the Boys with a proper nesting box, and gentle hands placed the little egg into the box. By the next day, there was another little egg. Soon there were two more and by the end of the week, a fifth egg appeared.

By this time the whole household knew the two birds weren't "the Boys" at all. This was a genuine set of mated Love Birds. The birds watched over their little nest of eggs with a fervor that was admirable. Both participated in keeping the eggs warm and safe.

Granny had been kept current on the events within the cage and was fascinated with the drama that was going on in her daughter's home. She started making regular visits. She watched as the little eggs were carefully sat upon by the parent Love Birds. Soon she received the exciting news that one of the eggs had hatched. And then another and another. One, by one, the eggs hatched into homely little bulbs of life. The parents cared for them in a frenzied way as the little bulbs grew and their homely little bodies became covered with gray fluff. Caring for five hungry little birds is an exhausting job. The constant feeding continued day and night, keeping those little mouths full. The parents were obviously tired, but they never faltered in their faithful care of the new family.

Soon Granny received the news that the gray fluff was turning into feathers, and a few days later, that four of the little birds' feathers were turning green while one was turning yellow. Both parent Love Birds were green with blue markings, so Granny turned to the Internet for research. She learned that the yellow bird was a Lutino, and that all Lutinos are female. Granny made almost weekly trips to visit the Love Bird family watching them grow and mature into pretty little birds. Within a few weeks, all five birds had grown into their full color and almost full size.

The Lutino who had been the last bird to break free from her egg was the smallest of the five baby Love Birds. As the days rolled by, and as birds will do, the larger four began picking on the smaller Lutino bird that had been named Butter. Granny's daughter decided that the four larger birds should be placed in a separate cage, leaving Butter in her parents' care.

The four green birds were perfectly content in their new cage because it was placed close to the parent cage; they continued to have visual and vocal contact with their parents. Butter was happy to be the sole recipient of her parents' attention. As she grew more confident, she became very demanding. She pushed herself between her parents, screeching when she wasn't the center of their attention. This behavior was disconcerting to the parents; they grew just a bit tired of the little yellow tyrant. It was time for Butter to fly away from home.

Granny was intrigued with these little birds. And her idea formed. She wanted a Love Bird of her own. Granny had a problem, though. She left home every morning and didn't return until evening. Love Birds are social creatures; they want constant care. In fact, they need constant care, and Granny wouldn't be able to give her bird enough attention to keep it happy. She had continued her Internet research to learn more about Love Birds, and she knew the only way she could have the Love Bird was to have two. They would entertain each other, and Granny's role would be as caregiver. It was a happy solution to the problem because the two birds would be so involved with each other that they would hardly notice anyone else. And Granny would have the pleasure of their cheerful company when she was home.

It was a happy solution for the parent Love Birds, too. They would be returned to their peaceful existence. Butter would go live with Granny. Granny would have company in the evening, and Butter would have a handsome green mate to cuddle with. Enough time had passed and the birds were old enough to leave home. The parents were more than ready for peace and quiet.

To prepare Butter for her move, she was taken from her parents' care and placed in a cage by herself. Selecting her mate was a bit tricky because Love Birds don't always like each other. They can be very picky about who they will, and who they won't live with.

There was only one way to find out which bird would be acceptable to Butter. Early one morning, a beautiful green Peach Faced Love Bird was placed in Butter's cage. This turned out to be a big mistake. The screeching and fluttering that took place made it obvious that Butter didn't like that particular bird. In fact, she disliked him intensely. So out he came, and later in the day, another beautiful green bird was placed in Butter's cage. Mistake number two. She didn't like him either. The third selection was just right. Within minutes, the two little Love Birds were cuddling, huddling and chirping happily.

Granny went shopping with her daughter and granddaughter for a cage. It had to be strong because two cats lived with her. Two Boots lived in the house and Norman Bates lived outside, only wandering into the house occasionally. The chosen cage was huge and perfect. It was large enough for two birds to have plenty of room to flutter around without feeling cramped. It was strong enough that it could not possibly be pushed over by a curious cat.

Granny had spent much time studying and planning just exactly where the cage should be placed. It would be in the living room against a wall facing two large windows. The cage couldn't sit directly in front of the windows because the sun would be too hot on the birds. Placed against the wall facing the window, the birds could see outside without being directly in the sun.

Granny was ready when the big day arrived for the birds' delivery.

When the big day arrived, the car drove up and an excited Granny went to greet her new birds. Out of the car popped her laughing daughter and chortling granddaughter, who greeted her with, "We forgot to bring the birds!" They had been so busy getting all the food and bird paraphernalia together and making sure all was packed securely, that they drove off without the birds. Neither of them remembered the two birds until they had almost reached Granny's house.

Granny wasn't disturbed by her forgetful family because wrestling the huge cage into the house and seeing to its placement was rather tiring. She could use another week to get accustomed to the cage in her living room. By the way, Granny had given Butter a new name, Maggie Mae, and Maggie's green companion would be named Shadrach. When Maggie and Shadrach came to live with her, she would be ready.

One week later, Maggie and Shadrach finally arrived in a small traveling cage. Granny thought it would be difficult to transfer them to the large cage, but she was wrong. They hopped in easily and within seconds were investigating their new surroundings.

Granny's daughter had brought a large supply of wild seed, bird treat, bird food, and cuttlebone. Careful instructions for all the different types of food were given, along with a list of all the fruits and vegetables that Love

Birds enjoy. Granny's, Maggie's and Shadrach's adventure had begun.

The very first "hands-on" lesson Granny learned about Love Birds is that they're incredibly messy. Seed, vegetables, fruit and feathers fly from the cage twelve hours a day. Thankfully, the birds sleep when Granny turns out the lights at night, and nothing flies out of the cage after lights out. The water bowl needs changing every time the birds poop in it—which is often. The food bowls need careful watching to make sure they, too, stay poop free.

Shadrach has learned that Maggie can be difficult to get along with. He's a mellow fellow, though. He sits quietly near her and doesn't let her rile him. When she's unhappy, he stays calm. He's the typical male, very stable and masculine. When Maggie gets frightened, she quickly flies to Shadrach for protection. She sits closely behind him until she settles down. He calmly nibbles at her head, picks at her feathers and winds his neck around her for security. It's a pretty sight. He knows, and appears to enjoy, his role as Maggie Mae's protector.

Soon after Maggie and Shadrach came to live in her home, Granny started speech lessons for them. The endeavor appears to be useless, but still she tries. Each time she passes the cage she stops in front of Shadrach and says in a low voice, "Hi Shad." She then moves to Maggie and says, in a higher voice, "Hello Maggie." So far the birds don't seem to understand, but Granny has high hopes. She'll persist and over time maybe they will speak. Who can say? They do watch her intently when she speaks to them. Sometimes they yawn in her face, but Granny won't be deterred.

One morning after shelling some fresh peas for the birds, Granny sat down to watch them eat. Maggie flew to the bowl and started picking at them. Shadrach flew over to share the peas but was met by shrieks until he moved back several inches to wait his turn. Maggie ate for several minutes, sending peas flying all over the cage and floor. While Granny watched this display of selfish messiness, Maggie ate her fill, turned to Shadrach and offered a pea to him from her beak. He took the pea from her and she scooted away, allowing him to eat peacefully. "Amazing," said Granny to herself, "how that little yellow bird completely dominates Shadrach."

Each morning as 5:30 a.m. rolls around, Granny continues to get up for her coffee, but the coffee no longer comes first. The birds are first with fresh water, fresh seeds, fresh fruit or vegetables and a bit of vacuuming to make the floor presentable. Next, music is turned on so the birds won't be lonely during the day. They listen to classical music while Granny has her coffee and gets ready for her day at work. The e-mail correspondents don't get quite so much attention now because the birds take up much of their time.

The last thing Granny does before she goes out the door is turn off the classical music and tune in a pop music station on the radio. Maggie and Shadrach are exposed to a good range of music.

The two birds sit chirping and whistling peacefully as long as all their needs are met. Fresh peas are a favorite for both birds. One Sunday morning, Granny decided to read the paper before feeding the birds. Their food bowls were sufficiently full and the water bowl, for once, was poop free. So she sat down, unfolded the paper and started reading the front page. Screeching and fluttering immediately emitted from the cage to a remarkable volume. A surprised Granny turned and watched for a few seconds. Maggie's little claws were clutching tightly onto the front of the cage while she screeched and Shadrach fluttered around from food bowl to water bowl making an impressive clatter. Granny thought they just might be communicating with her. Did they want to be fed right now? She got up, went to the kitchen, shelled a few peas and brought them to the cage, dropping them into the vegetable bowl. As she returned to her newspaper both birds ceased their clatter and quietly settled into their routine with Maggie taking her turn first and then giving way to Shadrach. Their behavior was so abrupt that there could be no doubt. The little beasts had erupted with their clamor insisting to be fed NOW. Granny had not followed their normal routine. She did, however, learn a valuable lesson—she needed to feed them immediately upon awakening.

Granny's knowledge of Love Birds grows day by day. They get sleepy as soon as it gets dark outside. She was delighted the first time she saw her little birds start to yawn. So wide were their yawns that she had a clear view of their fat little tongues. They sleep as close together as they can possibly get, climbing to the top of the highest perch in their cage. They lock their claws around the perch tightly so they don't fall off. Maggie and Shadrach sleep soundly all night until Granny wakes them. On the occasional morning when Granny gets up earlier than normal, the birds seem to have a hard time waking up. They sit quietly, not stirring for several minutes. They're creatures of habit and don't like Granny to change her routine—or theirs. On these mornings when Granny totters in early, the birds are slow and groggy, but their eyes are always open. She wonders if their eyes ever close. "Can they close their eyes? I'll tuck this into the back of my mind. I must remember to hit the Internet and research this."

When the two birds came to live with Granny, she noticed that they spent much of their time crowding together into a small bowl that had been provided for special treats. The bowl was small so they usually ended up one on top of the other. She thought it was a curious thing for the birds to do and mentioned it to her daughter. Within days Granny's daughter provided a tiny bamboo shack. The shack is large enough for both birds to sit in without having to sit on top of each other. They no longer crowd into the tiny bowl, but neither do they always sit in the shack together. Maggie hops in by herself and makes Shadrach sit outside. When he tries to hop in with her, she chirps loudly, puffing out her feathers so there isn't room for him. Shadrach usually gives up and sits outside the shack patiently waiting for his cranky yellow mate to invite him inside.

It's a strange relationship but they're content, so Granny tries not to worry. The birds spend most of their time swinging happily or just sitting close together on their various perches. They pass their days by chirping quietly and nuzzling. Maggie's and Shadrach's enjoyment in each other is a pretty sight, and Granny is content with their company even if they never learn to talk.

HOT, HOT vs. HOT

Be careful what you wish for ...

—HARPER'S MONTHLY (1902)

Satisfaction

Grandma had a small problem. Every morning, she made two cups of coffee. She lived alone and her coffee maker was large (it held twelve cups of coffee) because years ago her large family lived with her. Grandma knew she could continue making the two cups of coffee in the large pot, but something about an almost empty coffee server bothered her. This was a small problem, true, but she was troubled.

She finally found a solution to her small problem. While visiting her friend Shirley, she saw, sitting on Shirley's kitchen counter, a beautiful, small coffee maker. The capacity of the small pot was a mere six cups. Grandma was enchanted. She wanted one of her own.

Shirley cautioned her to be careful when searching for her new coffee maker, because hers made very hot, hot coffee, which pleased her. Most small coffee makers produce less than very hot coffee. Grandma was so excited by her discovery of the small coffee maker that she didn't hear Shirley's advice.

The very next day found Grandma in the shopping mall, surrounded by coffee makers that all had a twelve cup capacity. It seems that most people want to make large amounts of coffee in the morning. She went from store to store with no success. The shopping trip ended without a purchase.

Grandma left the mall disappointed in her failure. She stopped at a grocery store to make a few necessary purchases for the coming week. In the middle of the grocery store, she spotted a display of small appliances. Sitting on a shelf, surrounded by twelve cup coffee makers, toasters and blenders, was a beautiful, small coffee maker. It was perfection. She placed the small appliance in her grocery cart, saying to herself, "Oh, this is perfect."

Grandma was very pleased with herself and her new, small coffee maker. Did she go home and immediately make a pot of coffee? No. Grandma was thrifty and since she didn't drink coffee in the afternoon or evening, she waited until the next morning to try out her new purchase.

It may be difficult for you, the reader, to understand why a simple coffee pot was so exciting to this elderly woman. It should be understood that most folks who have reached an advanced age live very quiet, peaceful lives. There isn't much excitement anymore. Therefore, small things, such as a coffee maker that makes just the right amount of coffee, can be quite a "big deal" for them.

Early the next morning, Grandma woke at her usual early hour and bounced (well, not quite bounced, more like rolled) out of bed and immediately set about making her morning coffee. She measured two spoons of coffee, poured two cups of water, and pushed the "on" button,

and quickly the delicious aroma of coffee filled the kitch-
en. Grandma arranged the morning newspaper on the
table and poured her first cup of coffee. She was delighted with herself.

With her first sip of the wonderful smelling coffee,
Grandma finally remembered, with a shock, her friend's
caution: "Most small coffee makers produce less than
very hot coffee." Grandma's new coffee maker produced
good coffee and it was hot, but it wasn't hot, hot coffee.
Disappointment!

A Different Perspective

The small coffee pot sat sadly on a shelf in a huge grocery store. She was completely alone and very lonely.
When she was assembled, produced and packed carefully
into a colorful cardboard box, she knew she would soon
sit on a beautiful kitchen counter merrily dripping aro-
matic coffee for someone who would appreciate her
prowess as a coffee maker.

Instead, here she sat, pushed aside for other appliances, dusty and forgotten. Week after week went by and no
one had any interest in her. She knew her worth, but apparently no one else agreed. She hoped and hoped—but
nothing happened. She was very worried because she
knew that if something didn't happen soon, she might be
put back in that cardboard box, placed on a truck, and
shipped back to that huge warehouse. She hadn't liked

those cold, empty days waiting to be taken to a busy grocery store and placed where she could be seen. Why, oh why, was she so unwanted?

Every day, all day long, people, mostly women, walked past her without even a glance. They did stop and look at all the other appliances. Those appliances, for the most part, didn't stay on the shelves long. They were touched, admired, and placed in a shopping cart to be taken home and put to use doing what they were made to do. Why did no one touch and admire her? She was shiny and beautiful. She knew how to make very good coffee, but week after week, here she sat. Why, oh why was she unwanted and unused?

Early one morning, when she had almost given up hope of ever being appreciated, a wonderful thing happened. A little old woman stopped in front of her and exclaimed happily, "Oh, this is perfect." She was taken off the shelf, touched, admired, placed in her cardboard box and carefully set down in a shopping cart. At last, she was going home and would be making pot after pot of coffee for someone. Her mission in life was finally starting. The little coffee maker enjoyed being pushed up and down the grocery aisles. She shared her ride with carrots and apples and frozen boxes of food. She thoroughly enjoyed being placed onto a moving conveyor belt, with the groceries in her cart. The moving surface tickled her bottom. She was placed in a large bag and for a while, the atmosphere turned dark and stifling. The sensation of moving was interesting, and the hum of a motor almost put her to sleep, but not quite.

Soon she was placed on a kitchen counter, just where she always knew she should be. There was an oven on one side of her and a stove on the other side. She had bright red canisters all around her. She was home and she was happy.

After an uneventful afternoon and a quiet, dark night, the activity for which she had waited so long, finally happened. Now filled with coffee and water, Grandma pushed her "on" button. At last, the happy little coffee maker heated and steamed and hummed and dripped, as only she could do, to make a delicious cup of coffee. When her coffee was, at long last, poured into a cup, she sat quietly and waited for the oohs and aahs that were sure to come. Disappointment!

Grandma sipped, swallowed, and turned, in surprise and sadness, to look at the new coffee maker. The little appliance was confused. She knew how good her coffee was. She had done her very best, and this was not the result she expected. How could grandma look at her that way? What had gone wrong? She listened and heard the disappointing words coming from grandma's mouth, "It's not hot, hot coffee." How could this be?

Grandma was troubled and this made the little coffee maker unhappy. What would grandma do now? Would she be put back in the cardboard box? Would she be taken back to the lonely grocery shelf? Would she be sent back to the huge, cold warehouse to be left forever unused?

Grandma poured a second cup of coffee and sat quietly. While reading her newspaper, she sipped from her cup. The coffee maker was emptied of coffee grounds, rinsed and dried. She was left alone to worry from her place on the kitchen counter. As she looked around, she saw for the first time a large, twelve cup coffee maker placed on the kitchen counter on the other side of the stove. "Not good," thought the little appliance. "Not good at all. I'm sure to be returned. If my coffee isn't good enough, I'm not needed here." All day long, she worried while she sat on her shiny, clean counter. Grandma glanced at her thoughtfully through the long day. But the little coffee maker wasn't used again that day to make her good coffee. All night long, she worried while she sat in the darkened kitchen on her shiny clean counter. As morning arrived she vowed, if she was allowed to make more coffee, it would be perfect for Grandma. When morning came, sure enough, Grandma stuffed her with coffee and water and pushed the "on" button. She heated, and she steamed, and she hummed and she dripped her very best. Grandma quietly poured her coffee and quietly read her newspaper. No comment. But the little coffee maker was eyed, unhappily, from time to time.

In all her short life as a coffee maker, she had never imagined that her product wasn't the best of the best.

The little appliance was humiliated and saddened. What to do, what to do?

These quiet mornings became her life. She produced cup after cup of excellent coffee for Grandma, knowing day after day that she wasn't appreciated. It was very embarrassing. She worked as hard as she could but she just could not make her coffee hot enough for Grandma. Her coils weren't programmed to make hot, hot coffee. They just weren't.

Living Together

The two, Grandma and the little coffee maker, lived together uncomfortably for some time. The seasons came and went: cold weather, wet weather, warm weather, hot weather and cold weather again. The seasons changed, but Grandma's dissatisfaction remained the same. She didn't return her little appliance to the grocery store. The little coffee maker hummed and steamed every morning with little happiness. It isn't much fun to work as hard as possible and still produce unsatisfactory results. Life went on.

There were periods when Grandma was gone for days at a time. During these interludes, the little coffee maker sat on her counter, sadly surveying her world. It was a pretty world, but she wasn't happy. She often had nightmares in the middle of the night, leaving her certain that tomorrow would be her last day on her shiny, clean kitchen counter.

One morning, long after the little coffee maker had become accustomed to her life, a surprising thing happened. She had been left alone overnight because Grandma didn't come home.

But Grandma was home the next morning and as usual, she stuffed the little coffee maker with coffee and water and pushed the "on" button. The coffee maker heated and steamed and hummed and dripped her very best and waited for Grandma's usual quiet reaction to her efforts. When her coffee was poured and Grandma sipped from her cup, the coffee maker was startled to hear Grandma utter the words she had longed to hear: "Oh, this is so good!" Grandma read her newspaper, sipping the coffee with a very pleased expression on her face. As she poured the second cup of coffee, she had a huge smile on her face.

The same thing happened the next morning—total satisfaction from Grandma with her coffee. Though she was happy with this latest turn of events, the little coffee maker was confused. What had changed? She had done nothing different. She had produced her very best coffee, as she had done since the day Grandma brought her into the kitchen and placed her on the counter. Grandma's apparently whimsical turnabout forced her to come to the conclusion that human beings are peculiar.

They Lived Happily Ever After

Grandma had spent the night at Shirley's house. Early in the morning, when she rolled out of bed, she went to the kitchen and, though the coffee maker was not her own, she automatically went about her normal routine of making coffee. She measured two spoons of coffee and two cups of water into the coffee maker, pushed the "on" button and sat down to wait for the process to produce her coffee. Grandma was about to be surprised. She had forgotten that Shirley's coffee pot made very hot, hot, coffee.

It was early and Grandma wasn't really wide awake. With her first sip of the coffee, she was shocked into remembering Shirley's caution that, "her coffee pot made very hot, hot coffee." Grandma burned her mouth. After a not very nice exclamation, Grandma finished her coffee by blowing before every sip. She did not enjoy the coffee at all. She did not drink the second cup of coffee. And her mouth hurt.

The following morning, back home in her own kitchen, Grandma had a totally new appreciation for her very own coffee maker that produced hot coffee but not really hot, hot coffee.

You see, humans have a nasty habit of thinking everything is greener on the other side of the fence. Most often, it isn't true.

Call it a clan, call it a network, call it a tribe, call it a family. Whatever you call it, whoever you are, you need one.

—JANE HOWARD

About the Author

A very imaginative fourth-grade teacher at Kit Carson Elementary School, named Mrs. Bishop, challenged Rachel to read several books in the Doctor Doolittle series. This ignited a passion for reading that continues to this day. Consequently, she could not restrain her passion from spilling over to these pages and sharing the countless adventures she experienced and explored, both personally and vicariously, over many decades. Rachel has lived most of her life in Southern California with her husband Ralph S. Costantino, and they proudly raised three remarkable children who've remained close by as Southern Californians. Most of her prose was warmly written for her six granddaughters' reading enjoyment. These short stories were written between 2002 and 2007.

www.ingramcontent.com/pod-product-compliance
Lightning Source LLC
Chambersburg PA
CBHW020335180626
46812CB00001B/214